She was impossible to resist...

And Conor was tired of making the effort. He'd been alone for so long, and for the first time in his life he'd found someone who could make him forget all the barriers he'd built up around his heart.

Somewhere in the recesses of his mind, a little voice—his cop voice—told him that spending the night in the same bed with Olivia broke all the rules. And making love to her would end his career. But at the moment he didn't care. "I want to stop, but I can't," he murmured, dropping kisses along her jaw.

Olivia sighed. "I'm sure there are rules against this," she whispered. Her tongue teased his nipple. She trailed lower, nipping and biting, and driving him mad with need. "And against this..." she teased, her fingers trailing down his belly, causing a flood of heat to rush to his lap.

He couldn't take it any longer. Grabbing her wrists, he lowered her to the bed and covered her body with his. "I think it's time we started making up our own rules," he growled. "And rule number one..." he said, raising himself above her, "is that there will be no more rules."

Dear Reader,

The offer was intriguing. My editors at Harlequin asked if I was interested in writing a trilogy about an Irish-American family. I'd just returned from a trip to Ireland and my mind was still filled with images of emerald-green hills, stone cottages and quaint pubs. So I had no problem at all coming up with the three sexy Irish-born heroes of my books—Conor, Dylan and Brendan, the Mighty Quinns.

Each one touched in a very different way by their harsh childhood, the Quinns have grown up without any feminine influence in their lives. So when they fall in love, they fall hard. Conor Quinn is the first to succumb. Always the responsible one, he turned to police work after raising his five younger brothers. But when he's asked to protect beautiful antiques dealer Olivia Farrell, his usual self-control vanishes and he finds himself caught up in a passion that may cost him more than just his job.

Watch for Dylan's story next month, and Brendan's the month after that. And for more news about my upcoming releases, visit my new Web site at www.katehoffmann.com.

Happy reading,

Kate Hoffmann

Books by Kate Hoffmann

Kate Hoffmann
THE MIGHTY QUINNS: CONOR

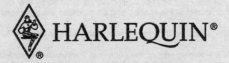

HARLEQUIN®

TORONTO • NEW YORK • LONDON
AMSTERDAM • PARIS • SYDNEY • HAMBURG
STOCKHOLM • ATHENS • TOKYO • MILAN • MADRID
PRAGUE • WARSAW • BUDAPEST • AUCKLAND

To Karin Vander Schaaf,
Who knew the answers to my Boston questions
before I even asked.

ISBN 0-373-25947-6

THE MIGHTY QUINNS: CONOR

Copyright © 2001 by Peggy A. Hoffmann.

This edition published by arrangement with Harlequin Books S.A.

Visit us at www.eHarlequin.com

Printed in U.S.A.

Prologue

THE WIND HOWLED and the rain raged outside the tiny house on Kilgore Street in South Boston. The nor'easter had battered the working-class neighborhood for nearly two days, the pleasant autumn sunshine giving way to the first sting of winter.

Conor Quinn tugged the threadbare blanket around his youngest brothers, sleeping three to a bed. The twins, Sean and Brian, were already half-asleep, their eyes glazed with exhaustion. And the baby, three-year-old Liam, lay curled between them, his breathing gone soft and even, his dark lashes feathered over chubby cheeks.

But Dylan and Brendan were still wide awake, the two of them perched on the end of their bed, listening raptly as their father, Seamus Quinn, spun another tale. It was well past eleven and the boys should have been asleep. While his father was away, Conor made sure bedtime was strictly adhered to on school nights. But Seamus, a swordfisherman by profession, stayed in port only a week or two before heading out to sea for months at a time. And with winter coming, his father and the crew of *The Mighty Quinn* would be heading farther south, following the swordfish into the warmer waters of the Caribbean.

"This is a story of your long-ago ancestor, Eamon

Quinn. Eamon was a clever laddie, so clever he could build a nest in your ear."

Conor listened with half an ear to Seamus's colorful tale, wondering whether he'd ever find a proper time to bring up Dylan's failures in math class, or Brendan's habit of pinching candy from the local market, or the immunizations that Brian and Sean still needed for school. But one subject *had* to be discussed, a problem his father refused to acknowledge.

Mrs. Smalley, their neighbor and regular baby-sitter, was up to a quart of vodka a day. Concerned for the safety of his three youngest brothers, Conor had been anxious to find another person to watch the little ones while he and Dylan and Brendan were at school. Social Services had already paid a surprise visit and he'd managed to hustle them off with an elaborate excuse about Mrs. Smalley's allergies. But if the social workers realized he cared for his five brothers almost entirely on his own, they'd declare neglect and send them all to an orphanage.

"One fine day, Eamon was fishing off the Isle of Shadows. As he passed by a rocky shore, he saw a beautiful lass standing near the water's edge, her long hair blowing in the breeze. His heart swelled and his face shone, for Eamon had never seen a more lovely creature."

Conor had every confidence that he could keep his family together. Though he was only ten years old, he'd been both mother and father to the boys for over two years. As Mrs. Smalley's drinking problem escalated, he'd learned to do the laundry and shop for food and help his brothers with their schoolwork. They had a simple life, complicated only by Mrs. Smalley's binges and infrequent visits from Seamus.

Whatever time Seamus didn't spend with his sons was spent at the local pub where he frittered away his take from the catch, buying drinks for strangers and gambling against huge odds. By the end of the week, he usually handed Conor just barely enough to pay household expenses for the coming months, until he and *The Mighty Quinn* chugged back into port with another holdful of swordfish. A few days ago, they were dining on week-old bread and soup from dented cans. Tonight, they'd enjoyed bulging bags of takeout from McDonald's and Kentucky Fried Chicken.

"Eamon talked to the lass and, before long, he was enchanted. All the village said that it was time for Eamon to take a bride, but he had never found a woman to love—until now. He brought his boat ashore, but as Eamon set foot on land, the lass turned into a wild beast, as fierce as a lion with breath of fire and a thorny tail. She snatched Eamon between her great jaws, splintering his boat into a thousand pieces with her giant claws."

Though Seamus Quinn wasn't much of a parent or a fisherman, he did have one talent. Conor's father could spin a beguiling yarn—rich Irish tales filled with action and adventure. Though Seamus always substituted a Quinn ancestor in the hero's role and often combined elements of two or three stories, Conor had come to recognize the bits of Irish myths and legends from books he'd sought out at the public library.

Conor preferred the stories of the supernatural—fairies and banshees and pixies and ghosts. Eight-year-old Dylan liked tales of heroic deeds. And Brendan, a year younger than Dylan, hoped for a story of adventure in a far-off land. And the five-year-old twins, Brian and Sean, and baby Liam, really didn't care what tale Seamus spun; they only cared that their da was home and their tummies would be full for a while.

Conor sat down beside Dylan and watched his father in the feeble light from the bedside lamp. At times, listening to his father's thick brogue, he could picture Ireland in his mind—the misty sky, the emerald green fields lined with stone fences, the pony his grandfather had given him for his birthday, and the tiny whitewashed cottage near the water. They'd all been born there, save Liam, in that cottage on Bantry Bay. Life had been perfect then, because they'd had their da and their ma.

"Eamon knew it would take all his brains to trick the dragon. Many fishermen had been captured by this very dragon and held prisoner in a great cave on the Isle of Shadows, but Eamon would not be one of them."

The letter from America had been the start of the bad times. Seamus's brother had emigrated to Boston as a teenager. With grit and determination, Uncle Padriac had saved enough money crewing on a longliner to buy his own swordfish boat. He'd offered Seamus a partnership in *The Mighty Quinn*, a way out of the hardscrabble life that Ireland promised. So they'd moved half a world away, Seamus, his pretty wife Fiona, pregnant with Liam, and the five boys.

From the start, Conor had hated South Boston. Though half the population was of Irish descent, he was teased mercilessly for his accent. Within a month, he'd learned to speak in the flat tones and grating vowels of his peers and the occasional teasing resulted in a black eye or cut lip for the teaser. School became tolerable, but life at home was deteriorating with every passing day.

He remembered the fights at home the most, the simmering anger, the long silences between Fiona and Seamus...and his mother's devastating loneliness at his father's endless absences. The soft sobs he heard late at night behind her bedroom door cut him to the quick and he wanted to go to her, to make everything all right. But whenever he approached, her tears magically dried and all was well.

One day she was there, smiling at him, and the next day, she was gone. Conor expected her to come home by morning, as did Seamus when he stumbled in from the pub just as the sun was rising. But his mother never returned. And from that day on, Seamus would not speak her name. Questions were met with stony silence and when they persisted, he'd told the boys she'd moved back to Ireland. A few months later, he finally told them she'd died in an auto wreck. But Conor suspected that this was only a lie to end the questions, just revenge for his mother's betrayal.

Conor had vowed never to forget her. At night, he'd imagined her soft, dark hair and her warm smile, the way she touched him when she spoke and the pride he saw in her eyes when he did well in school. The twins and Liam had just vague memories of her. And Dylan and Brendan's memories were distorted by their loss, making her seem unreal, like some fairy princess dressed in spun gold.

"So this you must remember," his father said in a warning tone, interrupting Conor's daydream. "Like the clever Eamon Quinn who drove the dragon off the cliffs and saved many fishermen from a fate worse than death, a man's strength and power is lost if he gives in to a weakness of the heart. Love for a woman is the only thing that can bring a Mighty Quinn down."

"I'm a Mighty Quinn!" Brendan cried, pounding on his chest. "And I'm never going to let a girl kiss me!"

"Shhh!" Conor hissed. "You'll wake Liam."

Seamus chuckled and patted Brendan's knee. "That's right, boyo. You listen to your da on this. Women are trouble for the likes of us Quinns."

"Da, it's time for us to get to bed," Conor said, weary of the same old cautionary tale. "We have school."

Dylan and Brendan both moaned and rolled their eyes, but Seamus wagged his finger. "Conor is right. Besides, I've got a powerful thirst that only a pint of Guinness can quench." He ruffled their hair, then pushed off the bed and headed toward the front door.

Conor hurried after him. "Da, we need to talk. Can't you stay in tonight?"

His father waved him off. "You sound like an old woman, Con. Don't be a nag. We can talk in the morning." With that, Seamus grabbed his jacket and slipped out into the storm, leaving his son with nothing more than a cold draft and an uneasy shiver. Defeated, Conor turned and walked back to the bedroom. Dylan and Brendan had already climbed into their bunk beds. Conor turned off the lights and flopped down on the mattress in the corner, drawing the blankets up to his chin to ward off the chill.

He was almost asleep when a small voice came out of the darkness. "What was she like, Con?" Brendan asked, repeating a question he'd been asking nearly every night for the past few months.

"Tell us again," Dylan pleaded. "Tell us about Ma."

Conor wasn't sure why they suddenly needed to hear. Maybe they sensed how fragile their life had become, how easily it could all fall apart. "She was a fine and beautiful woman," Conor said. "Her hair was dark, nearly black like ours. And she had eyes the color of the sea, green and blue put together."

"I remember the necklace," Dylan murmured. "She always wore a beautiful necklace that had jewels that sparkled in the light."

"Tell us about her laugh," Brendan said. "I like that story."

"Tell the story about the soda bread, when you fed it to Mrs. Smalley's wee dog and Ma caught you. I like that one."

So Conor spun his tale, lulling his brothers to sleep with visions of their mother, the beautiful Fiona Quinn. But unlike his father's stories, Conor didn't have to embellish. Every word he spoke was pure truth. And though Conor knew that love for a woman was a sign of weakness and trouble for any Quinn, he didn't heed his father's warning. For, in a secret corner of his heart, he'd always love his mother and that would make him strong.

1

THE SHOT CAME out of nowhere, shattering the plate-glass window of Ford-Farrell Antiques into thousands of pieces. At first, Olivia Farrell thought one of the display cases had fallen over, or a crystal vase had tipped off a shelf. But then a second shot rang out, the bullet whizzing by her head and embedding itself into the wall with a soft hiss and thud. Frantic, she glanced up to find shards of glass tumbling into the window display around a Federal-era breakfront.

Her first impulse was to throw herself over the breakfront, a rare piece valued at over $60,000. After all, the multipaned doors still contained all original glass! And the piece would be virtually worthless to her discerning clientele if it contained any scratches on the exquisitely preserved marquetry. But then, common sense took over and she dove for cover behind a rather overblown chaise longue in the Victorian style, a piece that might actually benefit from a few bullet holes.

"Oh, damn," she murmured, not sure what to do next. Should she run? Should she hide? She certainly couldn't shoot back since she didn't own a gun. She thought about locking the front door, but then whoever was shooting could just walk through the gaping hole in her plate-glass window. "Why didn't I listen? Why did I sneak out?"

Pushing up from the floor, she gauged the distance between her location and the back door of the gallery. But what if they were waiting for her in the alley? Since she wasn't familiar with wiseguy protocol, she had no idea whether her unseen assassins were determined to kill her at all costs or whether they'd regroup and try again later. Then again, they'd missed. Maybe they'd just meant to scare her.

"Phone," she murmured, reaching into her jacket pocket to pull out the sleek little cell phone she always carried. "Nine-one-one." She punched in the number and immediately began to pray. Perhaps she should just play dead, in case they burst into the shop, guns blazing.

Tears pressed at the corners of her eyes and her hand trembled as she waited for the emergency operator to answer. But she refused to give in to fear, pushing back the tears and summoning up her courage. She'd taught herself to control her emotions, to maintain a cool demeanor, but that was for business purposes only. Maybe a gunshot through the window was a good excuse for a little hysteria.

None of this would have happened if she'd just kept her mouth shut, if she'd just turned around and walked away that night a few months back. But she'd been scared back then, scared that everything she'd worked so hard to achieve was about to be taken from her.

The closest she'd ever come to breaking the law was fudging a few numbers on her tax return and ignoring the speed limit on the I-90. Now her business records had been impounded, her past scrutinized, her partner thrown in jail, and her reputation left nearly in tatters. She was a material witness in a murder and money-laundering trial against a very dangerous man—a man who obviously thought nothing of killing her before she had a chance to tell her story in court.

Olivia listened as the operator came on the line, then quickly gave her location and a brief description of what had happened. The operator asked her to stay on the line and she listened distractedly as the woman tried to keep her calm. Olivia had always heard that when someone came close to death, their life passed before their eyes. All she could think about was how she hated feeling so vulnerable, so dependent on some-one else's help.

"Just keep talking to me, ma'am," the operator urged.

"What should I talk about?" Olivia asked, her voice edgy. The only subject that came to mind was how quickly her life had changed in such a short time. Two months ago, she'd been on top of the game, Boston's most successful antiques dealer. She travelled all over the country, searching out the finest American an-tiques for her shop. Her client list read like a Who's Who of East Coast society. And she'd recently been named to the board of one of Boston's most prestigious historical societies. There was even talk that she might be asked to appear on the public television show *An-tiques Caravan*.

All this for a girl who'd grown up not on Beacon Hill, but in a working-class neighborhood of Boston.

But she'd risen above her rather common beginnings, leaving her past far behind and creating a whole new identity for herself—a wonderful, exciting identity, filled with travel and parties and influential friends. And financial security. She had saved only one thing from her childhood—an interest in anything one hundred years old or older.

"My parents were antique fanatics," she murmured to the operator, surrendering to the memory. "They used to haul me from auction to auction as a child, eeking out a living with a tiny little secondhand shop on the North End. We never knew where the next meal was coming from, never knew if we'd scrape together enough to pay the rent. It was frightening for a child, that uncertainty."

"Don't be frightened," the operator said. "The police are on their way."

"When I got older," Olivia continued, "they turned to me for authentication and I became an expert in 18th- and 19th-century New England furniture makers. My parents never had a very good eye for fine antiques and when I was just out of high school, they decided to try the restaurant business, managing a truck stop off the interstate in Jacksonville, Florida."

"The police are just a few minutes away, Ms. Farrell."

She continued talking, the sound of her own voice soothing her fears. As long as she could talk, then she was still alive and the fear couldn't consume her. "I stayed behind to attend college. I worked three different jobs for pocket change. I lived from hand to mouth for nearly my entire freshman year at Boston College, scraping to pay tuition and rent. I hated that. And then I found my very first 'treasure,' a Sheraton chair I bought for $15.00 at a tag sale and resold for $4,000.00 at a consignment auction."

From that moment on, Olivia had paid for her college education by buying and selling antiques. She discovered she had an uncanny eye for spotting valuable pieces in the most unlikely places—garage sales, thrift shops, estate auctions. She could tell a reproduction from an original at fifty paces and was a skilled bidder.

"Even though I majored in art at Boston College, I fell naturally into a career in antiques. I rented my first showroom space the year I graduated. Six years later, I formed a partnership with one of my clients. Kevin Ford was a man with money. I thought I had it made. He bought a beautiful retail space on Charles Street at the base of Beacon Hill." Olivia sighed. "How could I have been so naive?"

"The police will be there in approximately thirty seconds, ma'am," the operator said.

Olivia could already hear the sirens in the distance over the traffic outside the gallery. But even the police couldn't get her out of the mess she'd made of her life. She blamed herself for this whole thing. When Kevin bought the building, she'd had her doubts. Though he was wealthy, he certainly didn't have the millions to buy retail space on Charles Street. But all Olivia could see was the next stage in her meteoric rise to the top of Boston society—and all the business that would come her way.

Had she trusted her instincts, she might have realized that Kevin Ford's bottomless wallet came from underworld connections. That fact had been proved when Olivia overheard a late-night conversation between Ford and one of Ford's most important clients, Red Keenan—a man she later learned was a Boston crime boss who'd ordered a handful of murders last year alone.

The sound of more glass smashing made her jump and she prepared herself for the worst. But then a familiar voice brought a rush of relief. "Ms. Farrell? Are you all right?"

Olivia poked her head up over the back of the chaise. She waved weakly at Assistant District Attorney Elliott Shulman, the man in charge of the murder case against Red Keenan. "I—I'm still alive," she said.

He hurried through the shop and helped her to her feet. "This is just unacceptable," he muttered. "Where was the police protection I ordered?"

"They're still parked outside my flat," Olivia murmured, a warm flush flooding her face.

Shulman gasped. "You went out without telling them?"

She nodded, her spine stiffening at his censorious tone. "I—I just needed to get some work done. The shop has been closed for almost two months. I have bills to pay, antiques to sell. If I don't work with my clients, they'll go someplace else."

Shulman grabbed her by the elbow and led her toward the front door, his fingers firm on her arm. "Well, you've seen what Red Keenan is capable of, Ms. Farrell. Maybe now you'll listen to us and take his threats seriously?"

Olivia yanked her arm from his grasp. "I still don't

understand why he'd want me dead. Kevin can testify to the whole sordid business. I just overheard them talking. And I didn't hear that much."

"As I told you before, Ms. Farrell, your partner isn't talking. You're the only witness who can put the two of them together. After what happened tonight, we're going to have to hide you. Somewhere safe, out of town."

Olivia gasped. "I—I just can't leave. Look at this mess. Who's going to repair the window? I can't let the weather come in. These antiques are valuable. And what about my clients? This could ruin me financially!"

"We'll call someone to replace the window right away. Until then, I'll leave a patrolman outside. You're coming with me down to the station until we find a safe house for you."

Olivia grabbed her coat and purse from a circa 1830 primitive wardrobe next to her desk, then reluctantly followed Shulman to the front door. Maybe it was time to go into hiding. It was only for a couple of weeks, until the trial started. At least she'd feel safe again. When she stepped out onto the sidewalk, she gave her keys to the patrolman and murmured detailed instructions on the security code. When she finished, she closed her eyes and drew a long breath.

"Promise me I'll have my old life back soon," she said, trying to still the tremor in her voice.

"We'll do our best, Ms. Farrell."

CONOR QUINN knew the meaning of a bad day. Drugs, hookers, booze, smut—this was his life. Working vice for the Boston Police Department, he couldn't recall a day that hadn't been tainted by society's ills. He reached inside his jacket pocket for the ever-present pack of cigarettes, his own private vice, then remembered he'd quit three days ago.

With a soft oath, he slid his empty glass across the bar and motioned to the bartender. Seamus Quinn approached, wiping his scarred hands on a bar towel. His dark hair had turned white and he now walked with a stoop owing to years of back-breaking labor on his swordfish boat. Conor's father had given up fishing a few years back. *The Mighty Quinn* now bobbed silently at its moorings in Hull harbor, brother Brendan using it as a temporary home on the rare occasions he stayed in Boston. Seamus had moved on, using his meager savings and a gambling boon to purchase his favorite pub in a rough and tumble section of South Boston.

"Buy you a pint, Con?" Seamus asked in his rugged brogue.

Though Ireland was still thick in his father's voice, little of the Quinn brothers' birthplace remained in their memories. Yet, every now and then, Conor could still hear traces of the old country in his own voice, traces that he sometimes caught in Dylan and Brendan, too. But they were Americans through and through, all of the brothers had become naturalized citizens—save Liam, who'd been born in America—the day their parents took the oath.

Conor shook his head. "I'm on duty in a half hour, Da. Danny's picking me up here."

Seamus gave him a shrewd look, then set a club soda in front of Conor, before serving the next patron. Conor watched as his da expertly pulled the Guinness, tipping the glass at the perfect angle and choosing the exact moment to turn off the tap. He set the tall glass on the bar and the pale creamy foam rose to the top, leaving the nut brown brew beneath.

His father didn't bother asking. Though the rest of the patrons profited from Seamus's sage advice, over the years the Quinn boys had learned to handle their own problems without parental involvement. In truth, Conor had been the one to dispense advice and discipline to his younger brothers. He still did. Nearly his entire life, from the time he was seven, had been consumed with keeping his family intact at all costs and keeping his brothers on the straight and narrow. Making life safe had been his job, then and now. Now, he was just watching out for a city of a half million instead of five rowdy boys from Southie.

He glanced around the bar, searching for a diversion, anything to get his mind off the events of the day. Seamus Quinn's pub was known for three things—an authentic Irish atmosphere, the best Irish stew in Boston and rousing Irish music played live every night. It was also known for the six bachelor brothers who hung out at the bar.

Dylan was playing pool with some of his firefighter buddies, all dressed alike in the navy T-shirts of the Boston Fire Department. A bevy of girls had gathered to watch, sending flirtatious looks Dylan's way. Brian worked the other end of the bar this night and was occupied charming the newest barmaid. Liam had found himself a lively round of darts with a pretty redhead. And Sean stuck to the rear of the pub, dancing to the music of a fiddle and tin whistle with a striking brunette.

It was no different for Brendan when he was in town, finished with another magazine assignment or a research trip for his latest book. A soft and willing woman was the first thing he looked for. And though their father's warnings about women had been drilled into their heads from an early age, that didn't stop the six Quinn brothers from sampling what the opposite sex offered so freely—without love or commitment, of course.

But lately, Conor had tired of the shallow interaction he'd enjoyed in the past. Maybe it was his mood, the indifference he felt for life in general. Hell, the blonde at the end of the bar had been giving him come-hither looks for the past hour and he couldn't even manage a smile. Though a woman to warm his bed on this blustery fall night was tempting, he was too tired to put out the effort to charm her. Besides, he only had a half hour before he had to report to the station house—not nearly enough time.

"Good evening, sir. I've got the car outside when you're ready to leave."

Conor glanced to his right to see his partner, Danny Wright, slide onto the bar stool beside him. The rookie detective had been assigned to Conor last month, much to Conor's dismay. Although Wright was a good detective, the kid reminded him of a great big puppy, wide-eyed and always raring to go.

"You don't have to call me 'sir,'" Conor muttered, taking another sip of his soda. "I'm your partner, Wright."

Danny frowned. "But the guys in the squad room said you like to be called 'sir.'"

"The guys are pulling your leg. They like to do that to rookie detectives. Why don't you have something to drink and relax for a while."

Anxious to please, Danny ordered a root beer, then grabbed a handful of peanuts and methodically began to shell them. When he'd arranged a neat little pile in front of him, he popped a few into his mouth and slowly munched. "Lieutenant wants us down at the station house by the end of the shift. He says he's got a special assignment for us."

Conor chuckled. "Special assignment? Special punishment is more like it."

Danny sent him a sideways glance. "Lieutenant's pretty steamed at you," he murmured. "The guys say you're a good cop who just has a bit of a temper. Lieutenant says the skell is bringing brutality charges though. Already hired himself a lawyer."

Conor's jaw tensed. "That slime bilked an 84-year-old woman out of her life savings. And when she wouldn't give up her credit cards, he beat her within an inch of her life. I should have knocked his teeth through the back of his head and tied his arms and legs behind him. He got off easy with a split lip."

"The guys say—"

"What is this, Wright? Don't you ever speak for yourself?" Conor said. "Let me tell you what the guys are saying. They're saying this isn't the first time I've gone off on a suspect. They're saying Conor Quinn is getting a reputation. And that reputation doesn't help my chances of moving over to homicide. Combine the split lip with my other misadventures and the brass has got me pegged as a rogue cop."

"I—I didn't mean to—"

"You don't have to worry, Wright. It's not contagious," Conor muttered.

"I'm not worried about me. You've been waiting for an assignment in homicide for two years and there are only two slots open. You're a good detective, sir. You deserve one of those slots."

Conor shook his head. "I'm not sure I'm even interested anymore."

"Why not?"

He'd been mulling over that question for weeks now, but Conor hadn't been able to come up with an answer, at least one that made sense. "I've been trying to make this city safe for more years than I'd care to count. I honestly thought I could make a difference and I haven't even made a dent. For every hooker and bookie and scam artist I put behind bars, there's another one right behind. What makes me think I could do better with murderers?"

"Because you will," Danny reasoned in his own guileless way.

"Hell, I'm sick of playing it safe. It's time I started living my life. I want to get up in the morning and look forward to the day. Look at my brother Brendan. He chooses what he writes, when he writes, if he writes. He's living life on his own terms. And Dylan. What he does makes a difference. He saves lives. Real lives."

"So what are you going to do? You're a cop. You've always been a cop."

"Maybe that's the problem. I went from taking care

of my family to taking care of this city. I was nineteen when I went into the academy, Wright. I had responsibilities at home, I needed a steady job. Maybe I would have chosen differently. I certainly would have enjoyed going to college rather that taking years of night courses to get a degree."

Danny gave him a sideways glance. "You'll feel better when the lieutenant lets you out of the doghouse," he said. "He can't stay mad forever."

"So what kind of scut work does he have for us this evening?" Conor asked. He took a long sip of his soda, then wiped his hand across his mouth.

"Actually, it's pretty interesting, sir," Danny said. "We're protecting a witness in the Red Keenan case. We've got to transport the guy out to a safe house on Cape Cod and then keep watch for a few days. Kind of an odd place for a safe house, don't you think?"

Conor shook his head. "I guess they figure they can monitor everyone coming and going this time of year. One highway, one airport. Easier to spot suspicious characters."

Conor pushed back from the bar and started toward the door, Wright dogging his heels. He gave Sean a wave, then called out a farewell to his brothers. When he reached the street, he pulled up the collar of his leather jacket and turned his face into the wind. He smelled the ocean on the stiff, damp breeze and he knew a storm was on the way. For a moment, he worried about Brendan, almost two days late on a return trip from the Grand Banks where he'd had a last run with the swordfishermen before they started to work their way south. Why he'd decided to write a book about swordfishing, Conor would never understand.

Hell, swordfishing had been the ruin of their family life, the reason their mother had walked out, the reason their father had left the parenting to Conor. He sighed and cursed softly. Brendan could handle a storm at sea—he'd spent many a summer vacation making runs with their father. And Dylan could handle a fire out of control. It was Conor who was having trouble handling his life of late, making sense of it all.

His head bent to the wind, hands shoved into his pockets, Conor strode down the rain-slicked street toward his car, Danny hard on his heels. He glanced up when he heard footsteps coming his way, his instincts automatically on alert. A slender woman with short, dark hair passed, nearly running into him in the process. Their eyes met for only a moment. He glanced over his shoulder, thinking he recognized her. Bunko artist? Hooker? Undercover cop?

He watched as she slowly stopped in front of Quinn's, then peered through the plate-glass window. A few seconds later, she started up the steps, then paused and hurried back down, disappearing into the darkness. Conor shook his head. Was he so jaded that he now saw criminal intent in a perfectly innocent stranger? Maybe a few days of solitude on Cape Cod would put everything back in perspective.

The District Four station house was buzzing with activity when Conor and Danny arrived in the unmarked sedan. Conor was used to working the day shift, but days and nights would mean nothing now that he'd been assigned to protect a witness. Just endless hours of boredom, bad takeout, and what amounted to nothing more than baby-sitting.

According to Danny, the witness had been transported earlier that evening from the downtown station house. The lieutenant had been vague on the particulars of the case, preferring to speak to Danny and Conor in person about their new assignment—no doubt to use the meeting as a lesson for an unruly detective.

But when they strode into the squad room, the lieutenant's office door was closed. Conor checked for messages, grabbed a cup of coffee, then searched the mess on his desk for his pocket pad, the leather bound notepad that each detective carried for witness interviews. He remembered that he'd had it last in the observation room while he watched an interrogation through the one-way window.

He grabbed a pen and backtracked, finding the door to the room open. But his search for the missing notepad was stopped short when he glanced through the one-way window into "the box." The featureless interrogation room contained a single table with a chair on each side, a light above, and the mirrored window on one end, through which Conor now stared.

The sole occupant of the room was a woman, a slender figure with ash-blond hair, patrician features and an expensive wardrobe. He wasn't sure how he knew, but he was certain she wasn't a call girl or a drug dealer or a con artist. He'd be willing to bet his badge that she hadn't committed any crime. She lacked the hard edge to her features that most criminals acquired after working the streets. And she looked genuinely out of her element, a butterfly in the habitat of...cockroaches.

He stepped closer to the window and watched her for a long moment, noting the tremor in her delicate hand as she sipped at the paper cup filled with muddy coffee. Suddenly, she turned to look his way and he quickly stepped back into the shadows. Even though he knew she couldn't see him, he felt as if he'd been caught looking.

God, she was beautiful, Conor mused. No woman had a right to be that beautiful. He found in her features sheer perfection—a high forehead, expressive eyes, cheekbones that wouldn't quit and a wide mouth made to be kissed. Her hair fell in soft waves around her face, tumbling just to her shoulders. Conor's hand twitched as he imagined how soft the strands might feel between his fingers, how her hair would slide over his skin like warm silk.

A soft oath slipped from his lips and he turned away from the window. Hell, what was he thinking, fantasizing over a complete stranger? For all he knew, she could just be a better class of call girl, or some drug-runner's high-living girlfriend. Just because she was beautiful, didn't automatically make her pure.

Old habits did die hard. How many times had he looked at an attractive woman only to have his father's voice nagging in his head? All those cautionary tales, hidden between the lines of Seamus's old Irish folk stories. *A Quinn must never surrender his heart to a woman. Look beyond the beauty to the danger lurking beneath.*

He turned back to the window in time to see her wrap her arms around herself. Her shoulders slumped and then she rocked forward, her body trembling. When she tipped her head back, he saw the tracks of her tears on her smooth complexion. Conor's heart twisted in his chest at the fear and regret in her expression, the raw vulnerability of her appearance. She looked small and all alone.

Had she been standing next to him, she might have crumpled into his arms, hiding her sobs against his shoulder. But the glass between them was like an impenetrable barrier and he'd become nothing more than a voyeur. He'd never seen a woman cry before, except for the hookers he'd arrested, but those tears were usually just for show.

She cried for a long time while Conor watched, memories of his mother's pain flooding his mind. He knew he should leave and allow her the privacy of her emotions, but he couldn't. He felt as if his feet were glued to the floor, his gaze caught by her beauty and her pain. The tears had opened her soul and for a moment, he could see inside. He fought the urge to pull open the door and go to her. Whoever she was, criminal or not, she deserved a shoulder to cry on.

Conor reached out to turn the doorknob so he could enter the box, but just as he was about to open the door, he saw Danny Wright stroll into the room, a grocery bag in his arms. Slowly, he drew his hand away, stunned by the unexpected change in the woman's expression. The transformation was astounding. Almost instantly, the vulnerability vanished and her expression became cool and composed, almost icy. Surreptitiously, she brushed away all traces of her tears and glanced up at his partner, her lips pressed into a tight line.

Conor flipped the switch on the intercom, then braced his hands on the table beneath the window and listened to Danny's voice, crackling through the speaker.

"Ms. Farrell, I'm Detective Wright. My partner and I have been assigned to protect you until the trial. I'm sorry you've been waiting so long, but we've been making arrangements to take you to a safe place."

Conor sucked in a sharp breath. *This* was his witness? This woman who'd drawn him into her troubles with just a few tears and a stunningly beautiful face? "Aw, damn it," he muttered, throwing his notepad onto the table. He figured he'd be baby-sitting some wimpy little accountant or slimy two-faced informant. Considering his reaction to Ms. Farrell so far, spending the next two weeks in her company would be hell on earth.

"I don't understand why I can't just disappear," she said, a sharp edge to her voice. "I can go to Europe. I have business associates there who would be happy to—"

"Ms. Farrell, we'll keep you safe. There's nothing to worry—"

She brought her palms down on the table and shot out of her chair, the action causing Danny to jump. "I don't need you to keep me safe," she cried, her voice suffused with anger and frustration. "I can keep myself safe. I don't want your help."

Danny took a step back, caught offguard by the intensity of her outburst. "But—but we won't have any assurance that you'll return to testify."

"What if I don't testify?" she demanded. "Then you'll have to let me go, right?"

"Keenan will find you eventually, Ms. Farrell. Because, if you don't testify, he'll be out on the street and he won't leave any loose ends."

She gripped the back of the chair with a white-knuckled hand. "That's what I am? A loose end?"

Danny blinked, then shook his head. "Th-that's not what I meant. I was just telling you what Keenan would think. Listen, I'm going to go find my partner and let him talk to you. He's a good cop. He won't let anything happen to you, either."

Conor snatched up his notepad and stalked out of the observation room, straight through the squad room to his lieutenant's office. He wanted a reassignment and he wanted one now. He'd even settle for desk duty if that got him out of watching over this woman. Conor rapped on the door, then closed his eyes as he waited for an answer.

"Lieutenant went downtown," Rodriguez called. "The commissioner is holding some big press conference on his Cops and Kids program. He talked to Danny a few minutes ago. I think your witness is in the box."

Conor turned on his heel and walked back through the squad room, muttering beneath his breath. He met Danny halfway down the hall.

"There you are," his partner said. "Are you ready to roll?"

"Lieutenant's gonna have to find someone else for

the job," Conor muttered. "I've got too many open cases to take time off. Besides, District One should be handling this witness. It's their case."

"What? You can't bail on me now. I need you to talk to the witness. Her name's Olivia Farrell. Red Keenan's guys took a shot at her earlier this evening and she's pretty shook up. She doesn't want to testify. I don't know what to say to make her—"

"So let her take her chances on the street," Conor muttered. "If she doesn't want to testify, she doesn't have to."

Danny frowned. "What are you saying? We've got a chance here to nail Keenan. Besides murder and drug dealing, the guy's been running us ragged in vice. You should want him off the street."

Conor raked his hand through his hair and shook his head. "I do. But I'm not going to talk to her. She's your responsibility, Wright. You're the point man on this one. You get her ready to go and you drive her out to Cape Cod. I'll be in the backup car watching your ass."

"I gave her some clothes," Danny said. "Lieutenant figured we should sneak her out of here in disguise, like a suspect transfer. We'll drive past the South Boston station house on the way out of town, and if you don't see anyone on our tail, we won't stop until we get to the safe house."

"Sounds like a plan," Conor muttered. "I'll wait for you in the parking lot and follow you out."

Conor shoved his hands in his jacket pockets and started down the hall. Suddenly he needed fresh air, time to breathe. What had this woman done to him? With just one look, she'd sapped his strength and sent him running for cover. If he didn't know better, he'd have to believe his father's warnings were true. But this was just a job and he could certainly maintain a professional demeanor if he had to. Besides, as with all women in his life, the fascination would soon fade.

Consumed by his own thoughts, his gaze fixed on the floor, he didn't notice the figure who stepped out of the doorway to the box. She slammed into him and he grabbed her as she bumped against the wall. With a soft curse, Conor looked into the most incredible green eyes he'd ever seen.

She'd changed out of her designer clothes and was now dressed in a faded T-shirt, tattered chinos and a slouchy hat. An old camouflage jacket was clutched in her hands. If he didn't know her, he might mistake her for one of the vagrants who hung out down on the waterfront. Conor stepped to one side and, at the very moment, she made the same move. Twice more, they tried to get past each other, the two of them participating in some bizarre little tango right there in the hall.

Finally, he grabbed her arms and impatiently moved her against the wall. But the instant he touched her, his anger with her dissolved. Her skin was warm and so soft. A current shot up his arms, and as if he'd been burned, he snatched his hands away. "Sorry," he muttered.

"It—it's all right," she said. "It was my fault. I wasn't watching where I was going."

The sound of her voice surprised him. The intercom in the box had distorted it until she sounded like some harpy fishwife. But here, standing so near to him, her words were low and throaty, wrapping around his brain like a mind-numbing drug, immediately turning him into an addict for the sound. "No, it was my fault," he said, hoping she'd speak again.

"Can you tell me where Detective Wright is?" she asked. "He gave me these clothes to wear but I'm afraid they don't fit very well."

She glanced up at him again and he saw the vulnerability return to her eyes, the hard facade gone. "Detective Wright will be with you in a moment, miss," he said, steering her back through the door to the box. "Wait in here until he returns."

With that, he turned and strode down the hall, rubbing his tingling palms together as he walked. "See? She's nothing special," he murmured. "Just an ordinary witness. Sure, she's a beautiful woman. But sooner or later they all turn into clinging, grasping shrews." Conor repeated these words over and over as he walked to the parking lot.

By the time Danny helped a handcuffed Olivia Farrell into an unmarked sedan and roared off into the night, Conor had nearly convinced himself that his words were true. But as he followed the taillights of his partner's car, memories of the feel of her skin and the sound of her voice flooded his brain.

She wasn't like the others. He wasn't sure how he knew, but Olivia Farrell was different. Conor couldn't help but feel a small measure of regret at the revelation. He'd never really know how she was different, or why she made him feel the way she did.

The only thing he knew for sure was that he damn well didn't intend to get within fifty feet of Olivia Farrell ever again!

2

CAPE COD during an October nor'easter—Olivia Farrell couldn't think of anything worse, except maybe a root canal without anesthesia. October was supposed to be warm and sunny. But the sky remained endlessly bleak and the wind blew off the Atlantic, seeping through every crack and crevice in the beach house and rattling the single-pane windows until she was certain she'd go mad from the sound. The fireplaces throughout the cottage blazed but they did nothing to take the damp from the air. And the furnace, meant only to keep the pipes from freezing in the winter, did a pitiful job of staving off the cold.

She peered through a slit in the curtains, staring out at the restless waters of Cape Cod Bay, a sick shade of green and gray beneath the slowly rising sun. Rubbing her arms through the thick wool sweater, she fought off a shiver. How had she managed to get herself into such a predicament?

"Ms. Farrell, please stay away from the windows. We don't know who might be out there."

Olivia sighed. She'd been in protective custody for only two days, but already she'd had enough. She couldn't breathe without permission from Dudley Do-Right, the by-the-book cop that had been assigned as her shadow. Detective Danny Wright looked all of about fifteen years old, with a fresh-scrubbed face and a pudgy build. If she hadn't known he was a cop, she might have thought the gun he carried was a toy. Olivia ran her hands through her hair, then turned away from the window. "How much longer do we have to stay here? Can't we find a place with heat?"

"We're thinking of keeping you here until the trial."

"But that's twelve days away!" Olivia cried.

"We've got men posted at the airport, on the highway and even at the ferry landing in Provincetown. The only way one of Red Keenan's men can get past them is if they come over on a private boat and land on the beach. And with this weather, they'd be crazy to try. Local law enforcement knows all the year-round residents on this stretch of the Cape. This is the safest place for you."

"Then why can't I at least go out for a while? You said it. I'm perfectly safe here. We could go shopping, or go for a walk. Maybe get some breakfast in town?"

Detective Do-Right shook his head. "I'm afraid that won't be possible, miss. If there's anything more you need, I can send a man out. Books, snacks, whatever. The district attorney wants you to be comfortable."

"Fine!" Olivia snapped. "Send him out and tell him to buy me my old life back. I want my own bed and my cat and my hairdryer. My shop can't survive another two weeks of closed doors. My clients are going to go elsewhere. Will the department pay for all the lost business?"

The officer looked genuinely apologetic. "We're very sorry about that, miss, but you are doing society a great service by helping us shut down Keenan's operation."

She sighed then bit back a sharp retort and flopped down on the sofa. She knew she ought to be grateful for the protection, but she felt like a hostage, held against her will. Her incarceration would probably be much more enjoyable if she'd cut Detective Wright a little slack. "Since we're going to be spending so much time together, you might as well call me Olivia. I'm getting tired of miss."

"Actually, Ms. Farrell, it's best if we don't get friendly. Department policy says that we should keep our relationship strictly professional."

She grabbed the book she'd been reading from the end table. "I'm going to lie down. I didn't get much sleep last night." Officer Do-Right was about to issue another warning but she held up her hand to stop him. "And don't worry, I won't stand near the windows."

She closed the bedroom door behind her, then leaned back against it. The least they could do was put her up in a house with heat. It was probably warmer outside. Olivia crossed to the bed and grabbed her jacket, then tugged it on. In truth, she wasn't tired. She'd been so inactive over the course of her imprisonment she'd gained five pounds. Had she been at home, she'd be heading out for her morning walk right about now, taking her usual route, down Dartmouth to the river and then back again. She'd stop in her favorite coffee shop for a half-caf, no-fat latte, then grab copies of the morning papers, and head for her flat on St. Botolph Street.

Olivia paced the length of the bedroom, then turned

on her heel and retraced her steps. She picked up the speed and before long she was jogging in place. If she closed her eyes she could almost feel the brisk morning air on her face, hear the wind rustling in the leaves and smell the river in the distance.

But when she opened her eyes, she was still stuck in what amounted to a prison. Olivia glanced at the window, then walked over and pushed aside the curtains. The drop to the ground wasn't so bad. She could easily fit through the window without making a sound. All she needed was a little time to herself, some fresh air and exercise.

She reached up and flipped the latch open. Wincing, she slowly pushed the creaky sash up, the wind buffeting her face. The sound of crashing waves filled the room and she waited to see if Officer Do-Right would burst through the door with gun drawn. When he didn't, she threw her leg over the sash and wriggled out the window. The sandy ground was damp beneath her feet, muffling the sound.

Olivia turned around and pulled the window shut, then stepped out from the shadow of the house and headed toward the beach, avoiding the sight lines from the big wall of windows across the back of the house. The wind cut through her jacket and chilled her to the bone, but the sense of freedom sent her pulse racing and she wanted to dance and sing and shout with joy.

She ran over the dunes, through the wind-whipped sea grass to the hard-packed sand at water's edge. The roar of the waves filled her head and she jogged along the beach, drawing deeply of the salt air, caught up in the fierce weather. No one had ventured out this morning. Not a footprint marred the damp sand, no human for as far as the eye could see. "There you are, Officer Do-Right, I'm perfectly safe. Not a hit man in sight."

She wasn't sure how long she ran but by the time she sat down on a small patch of damp sand, she was breathless. Olivia knew she should go back inside before her watchdog noticed she was missing, but now that she was warm, she just needed a few more minutes to—

Arms clamped around her torso and she felt herself being lifted from the ground. The shock knocked the air out of her lungs and, for a moment, Olivia couldn't scream. She struggled to catch her breath as she was spun around and tossed over the shoulder of a dark-haired man dressed in a leather jacket and jeans.

He trudged up the dunes, carrying her as if she weighed nothing more than a sack of feathers. Finally, she drew enough air to make a sound. First, she screamed, long and hard, a shriek guaranteed to carry on the wind. Then she began to kick her legs and pummel his back with her fists. "Let me go!" Olivia cried. "This place is swarming with cops. You'll never get away with this."

He stopped, then hoisted her up again, adjusting her weight until his shoulder jabbed into her belly. "I don't see any cops, do you?"

"I—I'll make you a deal," she pleaded, staring down at his backside. She'd do well to keep her head about her. Surely she could reason with the man. From the look of his behind, he was young, fit, probably attractive. "I—I won't talk. I'll refuse to testify. Your boss doesn't have to worry. He won't go to jail. Just don't kill me."

She pushed up and looked around, then noticed they were heading toward the house. Officer Do-Right was inside! With his gun! Oh, God, she was about to be caught in a hail of bullets. And the way he was carrying her she'd be shot in the butt first. "You can't go in there," she warned. "The cops are in there. See, I'm on your side. I'd never say anything to hurt your boss."

When he reached the steps to the deck, he grabbed her waist and set her down in front of him, his fingers biting into her flesh.

Olivia swallowed hard, looking up at an expression as fierce as the weather. Even through his anger, she could see he was a handsome man—for a criminal. And his features were strangely familiar. She knew this man. "You!" Olivia cried. "I saw you at the station house. You're—you're a—"

An unexpected smile touched the corners of his hard mouth. "I'm the man who just saved your life. Now get in the house."

Olivia gasped, then narrowed her eyes. "You're a cop!"

He nodded once, dismissively, and she felt her temper rise. She let out a colorful oath, then drew back and kicked him squarely in the shin. "I thought you were a bad guy!" she cried, ignoring his yelp of pain and the little one-footed dance he did as he rubbed his bruised leg.

"Damn it, what did you do that for?"

"You scared me half to death! I thought you were going to kidnap me. And—and then, put a bullet in my brain or—or fit me with cement overshoes. My life flashed before my eyes. I nearly had a stroke. I could have died."

He stared up at her, bent double with the pain. It was only then that she noticed his eyes, an odd shade of hazel mixed with gold. She'd never seen eyes quite that color. Eyes filled with cold, calculating anger—directed at her. "Yes, you could have died," he muttered. "And I want you to remember how scared you were. Because that's what it's going to be like when Keenan finally gets you. Now get in the house," he continued, emphasizing each word. "Or I'll shoot you myself."

With a sniff, she spun on her heel and flounced up the steps. Of all the nerve! What right did he have to treat her like some—some recalcitrant child? Next thing, he'd be throwing her over his knee and spanking her. Olivia risked a look back as she walked in the door. Good grief, why did that notion suddenly appeal to her?

When she got inside, she found Detective Wright nervously pacing the room. He looked up and relief flooded his expression. Olivia almost felt sorry for him and was about to apologize when the door slammed behind her. "What the hell were you thinking, Wright? You never, *ever*, let a witness out of your sight. She could be dead now and then where would we be?"

Olivia turned and sent the dark-haired cop a livid glare, one he returned in equal measure, sending a shiver down her spine. "Don't you think you're being a bit dramatic? Besides, it's not his fault. I snuck out."

He took a step toward her and she backed away. "Did I ask for your opinion?" He turned back to Detective Wright. "Why don't you watch the road and the perimeter? I'll stay with Ms. Farrell for now."

"I don't want you here," Olivia said, tipping her chin up defiantly. "I want Officer Do-Right to stay. You can leave."

"Officer *Wright* is needed outside. And since you've decided to ignore his warnings, you're stuck with me. Or more precisely, I'm stuck with you." His gaze raked the length of her body and stopped at her toes. "Give me your shoes."

"What?"

"Take them off." He turned and stalked to her bedroom, then emerged a few moments later with the boots and loafers she'd hurriedly packed after the incident at the shop. "You can have them back once I'm sure you're going to stay inside. Now, give me your shoes."

Olivia had every intention of refusing but the look in his eyes told her otherwise. She sat down on the sofa and yanked both shoes off, then threw them in the direction of his head. Then she crossed her arms and sank back into the cushions, watching him suspiciously and waiting for the next demand.

He drew Detective Wright aside and spoke softly with him, giving Olivia a chance to observe him in an objective light. He stood at least half a head taller than Wright and his dark good looks stood in sharp contrast with Dudley's clean-cut choirboy features. When his face wasn't filled with fury, the guy was actually quite handsome—high cheekbones and a strong jaw, a mouth that looked as if it had been sculpted by an artist. His hair was dark, nearly black, and his eyes were that strange shade that she couldn't quite describe in words. Fascinating. Unearthly. Riveting.

While Dudley looked conscientious and trustworthy, this new guy had a wild and unpredictable air about him. His hair was just a little too long, his clothes a bit too casual. He had a sinewy build, long legs and broad shoulders and a flat belly that showed no evidence of too many donuts. When they both turned her way, she averted her eyes and casually picked at the fringe of a throw pillow she'd pulled onto her lap.

Detective Wright approached the sofa. "Ms. Farrell, I'm going to leave you in the care of Detective Quinn. He'll be with you until the trial. I hope you won't give him any more trouble."

She forced a sweet smile and slowly rose. "That all depends upon Detective Quinn's behavior. As long as he can stifle his Neanderthal tendencies, it will be pure bliss."

Wright looked back and forth between the two of them, then nodded before hurrying out of the room. Left alone with Quinn, Olivia wondered whether she might be better off taking her chances with Keenan's hit man. It would be best to keep Quinn off guard, to refuse to give in to his bullying. Twelve days of "yes, sir" and "no, sir" would be completely intolerable. She shrugged out of her jacket and tossed it his way. "You might as well take it," she said. "Do you want my socks as well?"

A muscle in his jaw twitched and he didn't speak for a long time. "I don't want to be here any more than you do, Ms. Farrell. But it's my job to keep you safe. If you let me do my job, then we'll get along just fine."

When he wasn't yelling at her, he had a very pleasant voice, deep and rich. His accent was working-class Boston, but there was something else there, a hint of something exotically foreign. "You said that you're being punished," she ventured. "What did you do wrong?"

"Nothing you have to worry about," he muttered. "As long as I don't lose my temper again, you should be safe." He wandered around the room, checking every window and door, then disappeared into her bedroom. She imagined him rifling through her bag, plucking at the lacy scraps of underwear and smelling her perfume. She could always tell when a man was attracted to her, but Quinn was impossible to read. He was probably telling the truth when he said he'd just as soon shoot her.

When he returned, he had a pillow and comforter in his arms. He set them on the back of the sofa. "You'll sleep in here tonight," he murmured.

"I sleep on the sofa and you get my bed? That doesn't seem fair."

"No," he said, "you sleep on the sofa and I sleep on the floor. We sleep in the same room, Ms. Farrell. If that doesn't suit, we can sleep in the same bed. That's up to you. I just need to be able to get to you quickly."

Olivia scowled. "Listen, Quinn, I—"

"Conor," he interrupted. "You can call me Conor. And there's no use arguing. I'm not going to change my mind."

Olivia opened her mouth to protest, then snapped it shut. She'd never felt entirely safe with Detective Wright. But with Conor Quinn, there was no doubt in her mind that he'd do what he had to do to protect her, regardless of her feelings in the matter. When he'd grabbed her on the beach, she had to admit she'd been scared. What if he *had* been one of Keenan's men? Chances were she'd be floating facedown in the bay right about now.

"I'm going to make a fresh pot of coffee," she said grudgingly. "Would you like a cup?" He nodded, but when she got up, he followed her into the kitchen. He methodically checked the windows and doors, then sat down on a stool at the breakfast bar. "Are you going to follow me around all day?" she asked as she filled the pot with cold water.

"If I have to," he said. His shrewd gaze skimmed over her body, blatantly, as if he were trying to see right through her clothes. "Why did you climb out the window?"

Olivia sighed. "You have to understand that I'm used to my own space, my own life. I never wanted this, never wanted to get involved. I shouldn't be here."

"But you are involved," he murmured, his eyes probing, his expression curious.

"I tried to explain to the district attorney that I didn't want to testify but—"

"Ms. Farrell, you have a duty to do what's right. Red Keenan is scum, a big player in the mob. With your testimony, we can put him away. A little inconvenience on your part is nothing compared to the pain that man has caused countless innocent people." With that, he pushed away from the counter and walked out of the room. "And stay away from the windows," he called.

The rest of the day passed in excruciating boredom. She stayed away from the windows and out of Conor Quinn's way. And he stayed just close enough to make her uneasy. Whenever she looked at him, he was watching her, silently, intently. Olivia assumed he was waiting for her to make another run for freedom. But she'd already resigned herself to her fate. The trial was twelve days away—twelve long days spent in the company of the brooding Conor Quinn. She'd need to choose her fights carefully if she expected to survive.

THE SMELLS coming from the kitchen were too much to resist. Conor glanced up from an old issue of *Sports Illustrated,* then levered himself up from the overstuffed chair he'd occupied for the past hour. Furrowing his hands through his hair, he wandered into the kitchen to find pots bubbling on the stove and Olivia Farrell busily chopping vegetables.

"Smells good," he said.

She looked up at him for a brief moment, then turned her attention back to the salad she was preparing. "I asked Detective Wright for some groceries yesterday. I was getting a little tired of take-out meals and a little angry with my situation, so I made the grocery list as complicated as I could."

He slid onto the kitchen stool. "What are you making?"

"Paella," she said.

"What?"

"It's an Italian seafood stew. They probably had fits trying to hunt down fresh shrimp and scallops. But then, I could afford to wait. I've got plenty of time, which is what it takes to make paella, and it's always better the second day." She looked at him again, this time letting her gaze linger for a long moment. Olivia Farrell had very alluring eyes, Conor concluded. Wide and trusting, ringed with thick lashes. She didn't wear much makeup, allowing her natural beauty to shine through. "There's a bottle of wine in the fridge. You can open it, if you like."

"I shouldn't drink on duty," Conor said, reaching for the wine.

Olivia managed a tiny smile. "I promise I won't try to escape again. You can have a small glass, can't you?" She reached into a cabinet next to the sink and pulled out two wine goblets, then set them down in front of him.

Had this evening occurred under different circumstances, Conor could imagine them on a first date—Olivia cooking dinner for him at her apartment, Conor bringing the wine. He grabbed the bottle, then took the corkscrew and opened it. Perhaps if he thought of this as a personal rather than a professional relationship, it might be much more tolerable. "Do you like to cook?"

Olivia shrugged. "I don't cook often," she said, "at least not like this. It's kind of silly to cook for one."

"Then you don't have a..." He let his question drift off. Maybe that was getting too personal.

"A boyfriend?" She shook her head. "Not right now. How about you?"

He smiled. "No boyfriend for me either."

She glanced up, then giggled softly. "I meant, do you have a girlfriend? Or maybe a wife?"

He poured her a generous glass of wine, then

splashed a bit into a goblet for himself. He wasn't much of a wine drinker, but he had to admit that the crisp Chardonnay tasted good. "Cops don't make good husbands."

She reached for her glass, then took a sip as she studied him shrewdly. "The accent," she said. "I can't place it."

"Southside Boston, with a dash of County Cork," Conor replied. "I was born in Ireland."

She raised her eyebrow. "When did you leave?"

"Twenty-seven years ago. I was six." Conor hated talking about himself. His life had been so ordinary, of no interest to a sophisticated woman like Olivia Farrell. "Where are you from, Ms. Farrell?" he asked, deftly changing the subject.

"Olivia," she said. "I've lived in Boston all my life."

A long silence grew between them as he watched her preparing the meal. She moved with such grace, everything she did seemed like part of a dance and Conor found himself fascinated by the turn of her head or the flutter of her fingers. Even though she was casually dressed in a bulky cable-knit sweater and jeans, elegance and class seemed to radiate from her body.

"What made you become a cop?" she asked, interrupting his thoughts.

Conor pushed up from the stool and circled around the counter to peer into the pot she was stirring. "It's a long story," he said.

"Like I said, I've got plenty of time. Twelve days, in fact. Which is good, because trying to carry on a conversation with the likes of you is like talking to a—a bowl of vegetables."

Conor chuckled. "I guess I don't talk much."

"Ah, a sentence with more than five words," she said sarcastically. "We're making progress. Before the night is out, I expect scintillating repartee."

She dipped a spoon into the pot and tasted the sauce. Then she held out the spoon to him. He took her hand and steadied it as he licked the end of the spoon. The feel of her tiny wrist, her soft skin beneath his fingertips, sent a frisson of electricity up his arm.

Their eyes met and, for a long moment, neither one of them moved. Had it been a first date, Conor may have taken the spoon from her hand and swept her slender body into his arms, kissing her until he lost himself in the taste of her mouth and the feel of her soft flesh.

But this was not a first date, he reminded himself. He was a cop, charged with protecting a witness. And fantasizing about this witness, no matter how beautiful she was, would only take his mind off the real dangers that waited for her outside the beach cottage. He drew back, forcing his gaze to fix on a spot over her shoulder. "I should go check everything outside before it gets dark," he murmured, schooling his voice into indifference. "Make sure Danny hasn't fallen asleep."

He strode to the kitchen door, not bothering to fetch his jacket from the other room. The icy air would do him good, clear his head. "Don't go near the windows," he said as he stepped outside.

Conor waved at his partner, stationed in a parked car near the road. He was tempted to switch jobs again with the poor guy. To give him paella and fine wine in turn for endless hours of lukewarm coffee, stale donuts and talk radio. Conor had always taken his job seriously, but it was hard to think about work while sitting in the same room as Olivia Farrell. Why did she have to be so beautiful?

He'd flipped through the case file in the car, but hadn't really bothered to read it in detail. In truth, he didn't want to know more about Olivia Farrell. He already knew she was attractive and desirable and intriguing. But after spending the afternoon in her presence, his curiosity had been piqued. Right now, he wanted to know every detail he could about her and her involvement with Red Keenan.

Maybe, after that, he could start looking at her as just a witness and stop thinking of her as a beautiful woman.

THE LIGHT from the fire had waned and Conor rose from the floor to poke at the embers. Outside the wind howled and shrieked, waves crashing against the shore. He'd watched the weather reports earlier in the day and knew the nor'easter was blowing itself out. He thought again about Brendan, wondering if he'd put into port yet. The only solace he could find in the storm was that Keenan's men wouldn't dare to venture outside.

Inside the beach house, the remains of dinner were scattered across the coffee table, dirty bowls, half-eaten bread, and the empty bottle of wine. Conor glanced over at the sofa. Olivia Farrell lay curled up asleep beneath a soft afghan, her hands clutched beneath her chin. He recalled a picture he'd found in one of his Irish storybooks, a drawing of Derdriu, an ancient beauty, betrothed to a king yet loved by a common warrior. Olivia's hair, like Derdriu's, was a pale shade of gold. The waves and curls spread over the pillow and her perfect skin shone like porcelain in the dim light from the fire.

He tossed another log on the fire. Sparks scattered across the hearth and the log popped and sizzled before it caught fire. His father had often told the tale of how Derdriu's beauty had brought only death and destruction to her people. But Conor remembered the drawing, how sweet and vulnerable her face had looked to his ten-year-old eyes. Even then, he'd doubted his father's warnings about the opposite sex.

He'd been sent to protect this woman, been asked to lay his life on the line for her like some ancient warrior. Yet what did he really know about her? Conor crossed the room and pulled the copy of the police file from his duffel bag. Then he wandered back to the fire, drawing nearer to the light to read. From what he could tell, Olivia Farrell was an ordinary citizen, caught up in extraordinary circumstances.

Her partner, Kevin Ford, had been arrested for participating in a money-laundering scheme for organized crime boss Red Keenan, a scheme that had included murder. The mechanics of the scheme were quite complex—buying expensive antiques for Keenan, reselling them to bogus clients for three or four times the value, then handing over the freshly laundered money to Keenan.

Olivia hadn't been aware of the scheme, but she had had the misfortune of overhearing a conversation between her partner and Keenan, providing the only solid evidence to link the two. Conor looked up, wondering if she realized the true danger she was in. He also wondered what kind of relationship she had with Kevin Ford.

He flipped past the report of Ford's criminal activity to a photo of the guy. He wasn't bad-looking, Conor mused, in that polished, sophisticated, Ivy League way. A woman like Olivia probably found him endlessly charming…intelligent…sexy, even. Perhaps they'd been lovers at one time, maybe still were. Conor shoved the photo back into the file and grabbed the page that included a rundown on her background.

Olivia Farrell. Graduate of Boston College, lived on a nice street in the South End. No criminal record. Single. Twenty-eight years old. Co-owner of one of Boston's most successful antique galleries, Ford-Farrell Antiques. Well-known throughout certain social circles in Boston. Dated an investment banker, a corporate attorney, and a shortstop for the Red Sox. No long-term relationships since college. Both parents living, residing in Jacksonville, Florida.

Conor closed the file and turned his gaze back to her. "Stubborn to a fault," he murmured. "Possible potential as a kick-boxer. Sharp tongue. Great cook. Incredibly beautiful."

His gaze drifted down to her mouth. Though she'd worn a grim expression for most of the day, all traces of irritation had been dissolved by the wine and good food. They'd chatted over dinner, each of them revealing just enough about themselves to keep the conversation interesting. She'd told him about her shop, the excitement of finding valuable antiques, the wealthy clients she worked with, the elegant parties she'd attended.

He told her about the seamy underworld of the vice cop, the endless schemes criminals found to circumvent the law and the frustrations he felt when they got away with it. To his surprise, she seemed fascinated by his work and questioned him until he'd told her about the most interesting cases he'd ever worked. Conor sighed. He really shouldn't have been surprised. Olivia Farrell was used to sparkling conversation. She could probably make an undertaker sound like he was the most intriguing man on the planet.

She may be out of his league, but Conor still couldn't deny he was attracted to her, even though he'd always been drawn to women with more obvious beauty. Olivia Farrell's features were subtle, plain almost, yet so perfectly proportioned that a man couldn't help but notice. She looked…fresh. Clean. Pure.

He stood up and quietly walked to her side. Without thinking, he reached out and took a strand of her hair between his fingers. Startled by the silken feel of it on his skin, he drew his hand away then knelt down to examine her face more closely.

A tiny smile curled the corners of her mouth. She slept soundly, secure in the knowledge that he was there to watch over her. But could he really protect her against the power of Red Keenan? There was no doubt in Conor's mind that Keenan would risk anything to stay out of prison. He had money and power, and those two in combination could convince unscrupulous men that a favor done for Keenan would be handsomely rewarded—even if that favor involved killing Olivia Farrell.

As he stared down at her, so unaware, so vulnerable, Conor knew he'd step in front of a bullet for her. Not because it was his duty, but because here he could make a difference. Olivia Farrell was worth saving and, for the first time in a long time, he was proud of the career he'd chosen.

He reached out and gently pulled the afghan up around her shoulders. For a moment, she stirred and Conor sat back on his heels, holding his breath. Then her eyes fluttered and before he could move away, she was looking up at him. "Is—is everything all right?" she murmured, sleep turning her voice throaty and breathless.

He nodded, then pushed to his feet and walked to the fire. He heard her sit up, a soft sigh slipping from her lips. "You're worried, aren't you," she said.

Conor turned and looked at her. Her hair was mussed and her nose was red from the cold. She rubbed her eyes, then turned her gaze to his. "Not worried," he replied. "Cautious. This place may be secluded, but that can work against us, too."

"Do you really think they'll come after me out here?"

The fear in her voice caused a stab of regret at his honesty. "No," he lied. "Your testimony is important, but I think Keenan has more to worry about from your partner. Hopefully, they'll be able to flip Ford before you actually have to take the stand."

"Flip?"

"Yeah. They offered him a deal for his testimony

against Keenan. He's refused to talk so far, but as the trial draws closer, he might reconsider. If Ford talks, your testimony won't be that crucial. And Keenan won't have a reason to risk adding another murder onto the charges."

This seemed to reassure her and she pulled the afghan around her shoulders and lay back down on the sofa. "That makes me feel better," she murmured. "Thank you."

She closed her eyes and curled up beneath the afghan. For a moment he'd thought she'd fallen back asleep. He braced his hand on the mantel and stared into the fire. But then her voice came out of the silence. "I'm glad you're here," she said.

Conor smiled to himself. Strange, but right now there wasn't any place he'd rather be.

3

OLIVIA WOKE UP with a jolt. Suddenly, she couldn't breathe. Her eyes slowly came into focus and she found Conor lying across her body, his hand over her mouth, his breath warm on her face. She wriggled beneath him, but he refused to budge.

"Don't make a sound," he warned in a voice just barely above a whisper. "There's someone outside."

She swallowed back the choking fear that threatened to erupt in a scream then pried his fingers off her mouth. "What are we going to do?" she whispered.

He scrambled off the sofa, then handed her her shoes and jacket. "Put these on—quickly. I want you to go to the bedroom, open the window and wait. I'll take care of whoever's outside then I'll come and get you."

"Shouldn't we call for help?" Olivia asked.

He placed a finger over her lips. "I tried to raise the officer outside on my radio, but he didn't answer. If Keenan found you here, then we've got a leak in the department. And we need to get out of here as fast as we can. Now, crawl over to the bedroom and wait beneath the window. If you hear gunfire, I want you to get out as quickly as you can and keep running until you're safe. Understand?"

Olivia nodded and he smiled. Then he brushed a quick kiss across her mouth. His boldness didn't surprise her, merely made her feel more confident—and a little warm and tingly inside. "We'll be all right," he said. "I promise."

He moved to get up, but she grabbed his arm. "Please, don't get shot. I'm not sure I can do this on my own." She winced. "And I faint at the sight of blood."

He brushed a strand of hair from her eyes. "You'll be all right. If anyone grabs you, just give him a good knee in the crotch. That should give you a decent head start." A moment later, he was gone, disappearing silently into the shadows of the darkened room. Olivia waited a few seconds, gathering her courage, then slowly began to make her way to the bedroom. Her heart slammed in her chest, so hard that she was certain it could be heard over the howling wind.

She waited for what seemed like eternity, silently praying that the next sound would be Conor's voice and not gunfire. When she heard her name called softly from outside, Olivia nearly cried out with joy. She scrambled out the window and he caught her, carefully lowering her to the ground, his hands firm around her waist.

"What's happening?"

"I'm not sure. The cop that relieved Danny isn't there anymore. The car is gone and so is he."

Conor wrapped his arm around her shoulders, then led her out toward the beach. Only then did she notice the gun in his other hand. She stumbled in the wet sand and Conor took her arm and pulled her along. For a while, he led her one way on the beach, then they suddenly ran closer to the water and started in the opposite direction.

She could barely see her hand in front of her face as blackness engulfed them. Icy water soaked into her shoes and she tried to draw a decent breath, but Conor's pace was unrelenting as they continued down the beach. Every now and then, they stopped and he listened, staring back into the darkness. Then they continued on.

When she didn't think she could go any farther, Conor led her along a concrete seawall, then up and over a dune to a darkened beach house. The sound of breaking glass cut through the roar of the waves and she squinted to see him reaching through a broken pane to open a door. He silently led her inside, then closed the door behind him.

Olivia felt her knees folding beneath her and he reached out and grabbed her waist, his arm supporting her weight. He drew her body against his and rubbed her back to warm her. How could she feel so safe, yet so scared, at the same time?

"It's all right," he murmured, cradling the back of her head in his hand. "We should be fine here, at least for a little while."

"But we were supposed to be safe there," Olivia cried. "What happened?"

"I don't know," he said. "The phone was out and there was someone prowling around the front door. It could have been the wind and the storm, but I don't think so."

"I don't want to do this anymore," Olivia said, tears pressing at the corners of her eyes. "I just want to go far away, where no one knows me."

But if she didn't testify and put Keenan in jail, how

would she ever feel safe again? She'd spend the rest of her life looking over her shoulder, waiting for him or one of his henchmen to silence her for good. "I—I just want to forget I ever heard anything. You can't keep me here. I won't testify."

He placed his palm on her cheek, his grim expression softening. "Don't talk like that, Olivia. I'll keep you safe, I promise. From now on, it's just you and me. And people I know I can trust."

He pulled her along to the kitchen, then withdrew a cell phone from his pocket. Conor punched in a number, then waited. "Dylan? This is Con. I know it's late, but this is important. I need you to get a boat." He paused. "When did he get in?" Conor turned to her and smiled. "I want the two of you to bring *The Mighty Quinn* across the bay into Provincetown Harbor. If you leave now, you can be here before dawn. Tie up at the gas dock and make up some excuse for staying there—mechanical problems. Just wait and I'll find you. I'll explain everything then." He didn't say anything more, just hung up the phone as if his request had been understood without question.

He crossed the room to Olivia and rubbed her arms distractedly. "I need to go find us transportation into town. You're going to have to stay here by yourself. Just for a little while."

She shook her head. "No, I'm coming with you."

He considered her request for only a moment, then nodded. "This place has a garage. Let's hope the owners leave a car here during the off-season."

They moved through the dark house, eyes fully adjusted to the lack of light. The door to the garage was just off the kitchen and Conor opened it. He flipped on the overhead light and held his hand over her eyes to shield them. "Bingo," he muttered. When her eyes had adjusted, she saw a jeep parked in the center of the garage. "It doesn't have a roof or windows, but it has four wheels. The ride might be a little cold and wet, but we won't have to walk into town." He turned to Olivia. "Let's get some rest. We don't need to leave for a while."

"Shouldn't we find the keys?"

"If they aren't in the ignition, I'll just hot-wire it. Come on, my brothers will be here just before dawn. Hopefully, whoever's looking for us will wait until after the sun rises to continue the search."

"I—I don't think I can sleep."

Conor took her hand and laced his fingers through hers. "We'll get you warm and you'll feel much better."

They went back inside and he led her to the sofa. Then he sat down beside her and gathered her into his arms. How had they become so close so quickly? Olivia wondered. Was it the danger they faced, the two of them against the rest of the world? Or was this simply some police tactic to make her compliant with all his requests? Olivia closed her eyes and leaned against his shoulder.

She hadn't been touched by a man in such a long time. She'd had men in her life, but lately Olivia had found searching for antiques much more satisfying than looking for love. Still she'd never felt so close to another man as she did to Conor Quinn right now. How long had she been searching for this elusive feeling, the security of knowing that someone—even a virtual stranger—cared?

Olivia drew a ragged breath and tried to calm her chaotic thoughts. It would be so easy to fall for this man, she mused. But in eleven days, he'd disappear from her life and she'd be expected to put the pieces back together and go on as if nothing had happened.

She didn't want to think about the future. Right now, she could only think about the present, the next minute, the next hour. If she thought too far ahead, the fear would engulf her and she'd be too terrified to open her eyes, too afraid even to breathe. "Talk to me," she murmured. "I can sleep if I just hear your voice."

"Not a scintillating conversationalist, huh?"

She looked up at him and smiled. "I like the sound of your voice. It has magic in it."

"Then I'll tell you a magical story," he said, putting on a thick Irish accent. She listened as Conor wove a fascinating tale about a beautiful fairy named Etain. He patiently explained in a soothing tone that fairies, or the Sidh, were not tiny creatures with wings, but human size. They lived in a parallel world, a world that met the real world at times when one thing became another—dusk into night, dawn into day, summer into fall.

Etain had bewitched a king with her beauty, but when the king's brother met her, he fell in love with her as well. Conor filled the story with vivid detail, and by the time he had finished, she was captivated by the images he wove in her mind. Such a complex man, she mused. So tough and calculating on the outside, and so sensitive on the inside.

Olivia looked up at him. "How do you know that story?"

"My da used to tell us. He wasn't home much, so we'd try to memorize all the details so we could retell them after he was gone. It was like a competition between me and my brothers as to who could tell it the best."

Without thinking, she reached up and placed her palm on his cheek. He gazed down into her eyes and, for a moment, she was certain he'd kiss her. Olivia thought about making the first move, curious as to how he'd taste, how his lips would feel on hers. Would they be hard and demanding? Or gentle and tentative?

"We shouldn't do this," Conor murmured, his gaze fixed on her mouth. "You're a witness. I'm supposed to protect you."

Hesitantly, Olivia drew her hand away. She shouldn't have assumed he'd be as attracted to her as she was to him. Such a fantasy, lusting after her protector. And how silly that she couldn't see it for what it was—a way to escape the troubles of her real life. He was just a convenient man, someone to make her feel safe and cherished. "I'm sorry," she said, drawing away.

"Don't be," Conor replied uneasily. "It—it's pretty common. You're afraid—I'm...reassuring. It happens all the time."

"Then it's happened to you before?" she asked.

"No," he murmured. "Never."

"Well, that makes me feel so much better." She pushed up from the sofa. "I'm going to go find a bed. Wake me when it's time to leave."

She wandered down a long hallway, anxious to put as much distance between Conor Quinn and herself as she could. When she finally closed the bedroom door behind her, she leaned back and sighed. Everything seemed so unreal, as if she were watching herself in a movie. What had happened to her life? Just a few months ago, she'd been consumed with work, finding no time to even think about her pitiful social life.

And now she was tossed into the company of the most intriguing and handsome man she'd ever met. She should be thrilled. But the more she got to know Detective Quinn, the more she began to believe that Red Keenan wasn't the dangerous one. Conor Quinn was.

CONOR STARED out over Provincetown Harbor, scanning the waterfront for any sign of Brendan and Dylan. The sun was just brightening the eastern horizon and the weather had begun to clear. Stars were visible through the cracks in the clouds and the wind had picked up again, blowing from onshore. The tiny village was beginning to stir and Conor was afraid that they'd be sitting ducks once the sun came up.

He'd parked the jeep in the shadows of a fishing shanty near the docks, giving them a good view of the water and anyone approaching from town. "Damn it, Bren, where are you?"

"What if he doesn't come?" Olivia asked, her voice thin and tired.

Conor glanced over at her. He was tempted to draw her into his arms, to reassure her with physical contact. But he wouldn't be touching Olivia Farrell again. Not that he couldn't exert self-control; she was the one to worry about. He didn't need her mooning around after him, messing up his concentration and putting them both at risk. "He'll come," Conor said. "I called him and he'll come."

He felt her gaze searching his face, looking for some sign of the closeness they'd shared just hours ago. When she didn't find it, she sank down and wrapped her arms around herself, trying to keep warm in the chill morning air.

"If he isn't here in ten minutes," Olivia said, "I think we should leave."

Conor felt his temper rise. No way in hell was he going to let her start calling the shots! "I'll decide if and when we leave," he said in an even voice.

"I'm just saying that—"

"I don't need your opinion!" he shot back. Maybe his frustration came from lack of sleep. Or maybe he didn't like her questioning his competence. Or maybe he didn't like the fact that she was probably right. But once the words had left his lips, he knew chastising her had been a mistake.

"You seem to forget it's *my* life. They want to kill *me*, not you. I should at least have some say in the—"

Conor turned in his seat and faced her. "And if you refuse to listen to me, I might get caught in the cross fire. So, you see, it's not just your life. It's mine, too. We're in this together." At least until he got Olivia to safety. Then he had every intention of calling his lieutenant and getting someone else to do the baby-sitting. He'd make sure the cop was trustworthy, of course, but that would be the end of it. He'd rather face a year of desk duty than risk succumbing to the temptation of Olivia Farrell's body, her sweet lips and alluring smile at every turn.

"There's a boat coming in," Olivia said, interrupting his thoughts. "See it over there?"

The low rumble of diesel engines echoed through the crisp air and Conor squinted. As if by magic, *The Mighty Quinn* appeared out of the darkness. Conor had never cared for that boat. In his mind, *The Mighty Quinn* had come between his mother and his father, it had taken his father away from home for long stretches of time, and it had forced Conor to grow up way too fast. But he felt pretty damn happy to see her now.

Unlike Conor, Brendan loved the water and always had, using the captain's quarters on the boat as his home when he was in town during the summer months. During the colder winter months, he usually slept on the sofa at Conor or Dylan's apartment—or in the bed of his current girlfriend, lost in the throes of a weeklong affair that always ended when he headed out on a research trip or another magazine assignment.

The boat maneuvered through the narrow waters, then headed for empty dock space near the gas pumps. Conor took one final look around, then nodded to Olivia. "Come on. We can go now."

He stepped out of the jeep, then circled around to take her hand. They didn't run, just walked calmly toward the water, Conor protecting her back and keeping a wary eye on their surroundings. Conor counted on the fact that Keenan would post his men at the airport and along the highway. Extra personnel would be slow in arriving on the Cape. He'd never expect them to leave on a private boat. When they reached the dock, Conor pressed his palm into the small of her back, urging her forward.

Brendan didn't ask questions. He simply reached down and took Olivia by the hands, then drew her gently onto the deck of the boat. When she was settled, Conor stepped up and they pushed away from the dock without even bothering to tie up. It took no more than a minute before they were once again swallowed up by the dark, and for the moment, safe from Red Keenan.

The running lights from *The Mighty Quinn* were barely visible through the early morning mist that hung over the bay. The prevailing wind had knocked down the waves from the storm and the water wasn't as rough as Conor had expected. He glanced at Olivia, but she stared out at the western horizon, the salty breeze whipping at her hair, her face ruddy with the cold.

He wouldn't feel safe until the two of them were back on dry land, somewhere warm and secure. He wasn't sure where they'd go. His apartment was too obvious, and probably way too messy for guests. He might be able to commandeer Dylan's place, although his brother's housekeeping abilities weren't much better than Conor's.

He glanced up at the pilothouse, watching as his brothers carried on a quiet conversation. Whenever Conor saw Dylan and Brendan outside the confines of the pub, he was always amazed at how they'd grown into such fine men. He still thought of them as kids, the skinny, untamed lads he'd watched over. The temptation to parent them was still strong, to tell Bren he needed a haircut and a shave, to chastise Dylan for not wearing a jacket in the cold.

Though he'd never told them, he saw his ma in their faces every time he looked at them—in the striking bone structure and the thick, nearly black hair. He saw the same face in the mirror every morning as he shaved, but watching his brothers, so strong and well grown, he couldn't help but wonder what Fiona Quinn might think of them now. Whether she ever thought of them at all. Conor didn't believe for a second that his mother had died in an auto wreck.

When Dylan glanced over at Conor, he gave him a lascivious grin and low whistle, nodding his head at the spot along the rail where Olivia stood. Conor shook his head, then climbed up to the pilothouse. "Don't even think about it," he warned, stepping inside.

"Think about what?" Dylan whispered.

"What you're always thinking about when you see a beautiful woman."

"Ah, brother, a woman like that is obviously wasted on you," Dylan said.

"She is a pretty little thing, isn't she," Brendan added.

Conor growled softly. He wondered whether his younger brothers would ever grow up. Would they ever realize there was more to life than an endless string of women traipsing in and out of their bedrooms? "Just get us back to Hull," he said. "That's all I need from you two right now."

He climbed back down to the main deck and joined Olivia at the rail. She looked a bit seasick and completely exhausted. He gently took her icy hands and drew her toward the main cabin, holding her arm as she gingerly walked through the companionway. Bren had warmed up the main cabin and lights glowed softly around the spacious interior. Conor walked over to the galley and poured a mug of coffee from the huge thermos he found there, then held it out to Olivia. "Are you all right?"

She slowly sat down, bracing herself with her hands against the rocking of the boat.

"You'll get used to the motion," he said. "And once we're across the bay, it'll calm down. Have some coffee."

She took the hot brew and sipped at it as she glanced around. "It—it's warm in here. I haven't been warm in two days." She hesitated, then looked up at him with wide eyes. "How can you be so mean to me one minute and so nice the next?"

Chastened by her question, Conor turned away and fetched himself a mug. "It's my job," he said, stirring in a generous amount of sugar.

"Is that all it is?"

"What else would it be?" He faced her, leaning up against the counter and crossing his legs at the ankle.

She forced a smile. "Then I suppose I should apologize—for earlier. I didn't mean to get...carried away. It's just that my nerves have been a little frayed lately and I thought you—"

"It's all right," Conor said. He wasn't going to tell her that he'd wanted to kiss her as much as she wanted to kiss him. He wasn't going to say how much self-control it had taken for him to draw away, to resist savoring just one taste. Damn, he'd love nothing better than to forget all his responsibilities and do something reckless. To throw caution to the wind and drag her into his bed. But he'd already nearly screwed the pooch at the precinct. He wasn't going to give his boss anything more to use against him. An affair with a witness was more than enough to cost him his badge.

"Where are we going to go now?" she asked.

"Back to Boston—or Hull, to be more precise. After that, I don't know," Conor said.

She bit her bottom lip, her gaze dropping to her coffee mug. "If he found me at the beach house, then he's going to find me no matter where we go."

"I won't let that happen."

She drew a ragged breath. "As soon as we get back to Boston, I have to stop at my apartment. I don't have any clothes. We left everything at the beach house. And there's something else I need to get."

Conor shook his head. "No, we can't. It would be too dangerous. We'll buy you new clothes."

"Please," Olivia pleaded. "I've got nothing. My shop is closed, my apartment is deserted, I haven't slept in my own bed in days. I just want some things around me that are mine."

He didn't want to listen to her pleas. In truth, he was scared he'd give in. It was hard to refuse Olivia anything, especially when he saw the vulnerability in her eyes. All he wanted to do was protect her, but sometimes his instincts as a man were in direct conflict with his instincts as a cop. "I said no." With that, Conor turned and walked to the companionway. "If you need me, I'll be up on the bridge."

Conor cursed softly as he climbed the ladder back to the pilothouse. Dylan and Brendan both turned as he stepped inside, watching him with perceptive eyes. There were no secrets between the Quinn brothers. "So, what's going on with you two?" Dylan asked.

Conor shrugged. "Nothing. She's just a witness."

Brendan chuckled. "Give me a break, Con. We see the way you look at her, the way you hover. When was the last time you ever treated a woman like that?"

"Never," Dylan answered. "He treats her as if she's made of gold. Did you see that, Bren? Like gold."

"It's part of the job," Conor said. "If I don't keep her happy, she doesn't testify. Or worse yet, she runs off and gets herself killed and I get my ass booted out of the department for dereliction of duty."

"He's fallen for her," Dylan commented. "But he's deluding himself. Lying in lavender like Paddy's pig, he is!"

Conor forced a chuckle. Dylan might be quick to jump to conclusions, but he was dead wrong. The last thing he'd allow himself to do was fall for Olivia Farrell. Sure, he might be attracted to her. What man wouldn't be? She was a beautiful woman. But that was where it ended. "You forget. I was raised on the same stories that you were. I know what happens if a Quinn falls in love. Hell, I might as well just throw myself off a cliff and save everyone the trouble."

His brothers stared out at the horizon, remembering the tales of their childhood as clearly as Conor did. "I'm amazed we're not all psychologically scarred," Dylan muttered.

Brendan sighed. "Maybe we are. I don't see any of

us in real relationships. Something permanent. Something that lasts longer than a month. Six decent-looking guys, good jobs, straight teeth. What are the odds?"

In truth, Conor had wondered the very same thing. He couldn't deny that their father's attitude had something to do with his own approach to women. He remembered all the stories. He also remembered his mother and the pain he'd felt when she'd left.

Olivia Farrell could make him feel that pain again. She had that power. But he'd never let it happen. He wasn't going to fall for her, because as soon as they got to shore, he was going to call the station and get himself reassigned. Olivia Farrell wouldn't have the chance to bring this Quinn down.

OLIVIA WASN'T SURE where she was when she opened her eyes. She only knew that she was warm and that she'd slept soundly for the first time in days. Tugging the rough wool blanket up around her nose, she sighed softly. She didn't know where she was, but she somehow sensed that she was safe.

"Mornin'."

Startled by the sound of an unfamiliar voice, Olivia bolted upright. But the unfamiliar voice came with a familiar face. A strikingly handsome man, with the same dark hair and hazel eyes as Conor, sat at the small table in the galley, a newspaper spread in front of him. Her brow furrowed as she tried to recall his name.

"Brendan," he said, as if he could read her mind.

"Brendan," she repeated. Raking her hands through her tangled hair, she glanced around the cabin. "Where are we?"

"Hull," he said. "We put in about four or five hours ago."

She glanced at the brass clock above Brendan's head. It was nearly two in the afternoon. "Where's Conor?"

"He went out to find you a safe place to stay."

"And the other one, your brother?"

"Dylan? He went to pick up some groceries."

Olivia sighed. "And you were the one who drew the short straw and got to baby-sit me?" she asked, a hint of sarcasm creeping into her voice.

"As my da used to say, a wise head keeps a shut mouth." Brendan chuckled softly. "Or something to that effect."

Though the pressures of the past few days had dulled her instincts, Olivia could have sworn Brendan Quinn had just paid her a compliment. "At least someone wants to spend time with me. Your brother acts like he's been forced to take his pimply-faced cousin to the prom."

Brendan slid out from behind the table and rummaged through the galley until he found a coffee mug. "My brother takes his responsibilities seriously. Sometimes too seriously."

The offhand comment piqued Olivia's curiosity. She knew so little about the man who'd taken control of her life. Perhaps she could learn something from Brendan that might even the odds a bit. When Brendan handed her a mug of steaming coffee, she sat up, tucked her feet beneath her, and rearranged the blanket on her lap. "Tell me about him," she said. "Why is he always so grumpy?"

"Would you like some breakfast?" Brendan countered, avoiding her question altogether. "I can whip up some eggs and I think I have some bacon that hasn't gone bad. Dylan's bringing orange juice and when Conor gets here we can send him out for—"

"Conor is here."

Brendan and Olivia glanced up at the companionway to find Conor looming above them. He swung down the steps and stood in the middle of the cabin. Compared to Brendan's cheerful disposition, Conor seemed to suck every ounce of sunshine out of the room. Olivia raised her guard, ready to defend herself against Conor's bristling mood. "Brendan was just going to make us some breakfast," she said.

"I'm sure he was," Conor muttered, sending his brother a pointed look. "When it comes to the ladies, it's what he does best."

"Hey," Brendan protested, "I was just being—"

Conor held up his hand to interrupt Brendan, then turned to Olivia. "Come on. We have to go. I found a place for us to hole up for a while. Get your things and let's go."

"Things? I don't have any things."

Conor crossed the cabin in a few short steps then grabbed her arm and tugged her to her feet. "Good. Then we won't have to wait around while you put on your lipstick and curl your hair."

Brendan cursed beneath his breath. "You are a charmer, now, aren't you, Con. It's no wonder you have women fightin' over you."

This time the look Conor shot his brother was pure murder. Olivia decided it was probably best to go along with the plan, before the brothers came to blows over her need for breakfast. She smoothed her hair, then stepped up to Brendan, giving him a grateful smile. "Thank you for your hospitality, and for helping to rescue me."

Conor's brother returned her smile with a devilish one of his own. Then he gently took her hand and drew it to his mouth, placing a kiss on the tips of her fingers. "The pleasure was all mine."

Conor growled impatiently, then snatched Olivia's fingers from Brendan's hand. "Brendan is also known for his kiss-offs. He disguises his motives so cleverly that the women actually feel good about being dumped." With that, Conor pulled Olivia along to the companionway then hurried her up the steps.

When they reached the deck she turned on him, yanking her arm from his grasp. "You can stop bullying me now," she said. "There's no need to show off to your brother."

Conor fixed his gaze on hers, his eyes penetrating, his demeanor ice-cold. "Believe me, if I hadn't come back when I did, breakfast wasn't the only thing you two would have been sharing."

Olivia gasped at the outrageous suggestion in his tone. "Well, then I guess I'm lucky to have you to protect me." She started off down the dock, determined to put some distance between them before she hauled off and slapped that smug expression off Conor Quinn's face. But, a few seconds later, he fell into step beside her, alert, his gaze taking in their surroundings as if he were calculating the angle of the next attack, ready to put himself between her and a bullet.

As they walked along the wharf, past restaurants, taverns and bait shops, Olivia tried to maintain her indignation. But, in truth, all her whining seemed petty and childish. This man had devoted himself to keeping her alive and all she could do was complain.

Dylan was waiting for them, leaning up against the side of a red Mustang. He handed the keys to Conor, then opened the passenger door for Olivia. "If I find one dent, one scratch," he warned Conor, "I'll hunt you down."

When she and Conor were both inside, she turned to him, anxious to set things straight between them, but his jaw was set and his expression so distant that the words died in her throat. And by the time they reached the motel on the highway to Cohasset, she was afraid to say anything to him at all.

Conor helped her out of the car, then reached in his pocket and withdrew a room key. When he opened the door and stepped aside, Olivia got a chance to see how low her life had sunk. The room was straight out of a bad movie, with a lumpy iron bed shoved up against the wall and faded wallpaper in putrid shades of orange and avocado green. The linoleum floor was scarred with cigarette burns and the room smelled of stale smoke and mildew. She slowly walked to the bathroom, afraid of what she might find there. But the bathroom was surprisingly clean, the old fixtures had been scrubbed white and smelled of strong disinfectant.

"It's not a palace," Conor murmured. "But we'll be safe here for now. And if we need to make a run for it, Brendan's boat is just a few miles away."

Olivia turned to him and forced a smile. "I'm sorry," she said. "I don't mean to seem ungrateful."

He stared down at his shoes, then shrugged. "And I don't mean to be so dictatorial. It's just hard when you fight me on this. I know Red Keenan and he'll stop at nothing to keep you from testifying."

"I feel like my life has been taken away from me. All I have are the clothes I'm wearing. I'm worried—about my business, about my apartment, about Tommy."

She'd worried how her cat was surviving with her landlady. Usually Mrs. Callahan cared for the cat in Olivia's apartment, but Olivia had been afraid if anyone broke in, Tommy would make his escape and be left to fend for himself on the street. A notorious cat hater, Mrs. Callahan had reluctantly agreed to take the cat in trade for an addition to her huge collection of Hummel figurines. And though Olivia didn't usually deal in Hummel pieces, she quickly agreed.

"Tommy?"

"I left him with my landlady," Olivia explained. "She lives just down the street. I just didn't want him to get mixed up in this. And she's taken care of him before. I just wish he were here with me. I'd sleep better if I knew he was safe."

Conor stared at her for a long moment, his mouth agape. "You have a kid? And you didn't tell the police about this?" He turned away from her and began to pace the room.

Olivia opened her mouth to correct his assumption, then reconsidered the impulse. "Tommy is everything to me," she said, careful with her words so she wouldn't tell an outright lie. "I'm just so worried that Red Keenan might find out about him and..." She let her voice trail off. If she couldn't have her own clothes and she couldn't sleep in her own bed, she could at least have her cat!

"I have to go get him," Conor said. "He won't be safe if he isn't with us. How old is he?"

"Nine," Olivia replied.

"What about his father?" Conor asked. "Isn't he around?"

His direct gaze told her that his question was more than just a matter of police business. He wanted to know whether she shared a passionate relationship with another man. "He's out of the picture. He was kind of a...tomcat." A flood of guilt washed over her. She really should tell him the truth! But she'd been bullied and badgered enough over the past few days. It felt good to exert a small measure of control.

Conor reached into his jacket pocket and pulled out his car keys. "I'm going to go get him." He strode over to the phone and picked it up, then held it out to her. "I want you to call your landlady and tell her I'm on the way. One phone call and keep it short. Don't answer any questions, understand? What's her address?"

Olivia told him and he wrote it down in a little notebook he kept in his jacket pocket. "She'll be happy to see you," Olivia explained. "She'll be glad to have Tommy out of her hair."

He shook his head again, as if he couldn't quite get his mind around the notion that she was a mother. "Geez, Olivia, why didn't you say something?"

Olivia managed a contrite shrug and took the phone from his hands. To her surprise, he reached up and touched her cheek with his palm. Another wave of guilt consumed her. "Conor, you don't have to—"

He pressed a finger to her lips. "I'll be all right," he said. "I can sneak in and sneak out without anyone noticing. If Keenan's men are watching your flat, they'll never see me or Tommy. You'll stay on the boat with Brendan while I'm gone."

"But I thought I was safe here. And—well, I was looking forward to a hot shower. I promise I won't budge from this room."

He considered her request for a long moment, then agreed by giving her a brief but potent kiss. Olivia stared up at him and saw that the impulse had taken him by surprise. He cleared his throat and forced a smile. "I'm still going to ask Brendan to keep an eye on things outside."

Olivia winced. This had gone entirely too far! She had to tell him that Tommy was her cat, not her son. But she'd been on the receiving end of his anger enough for one day. She'd just have to take her chances when he returned. "Are you positive you'll be all right?"

He nodded, then turned for the door. When it closed behind him, Olivia's hand came to her mouth and she touched her lips. They were still warm and damp from his kiss. "If he gets shot, you'll never be able to forgive yourself."

But then Conor wouldn't get shot. He wouldn't allow it. He was brave and strong and clever. And when he returned he'd be seething with anger. But he wouldn't desert her, no matter what she did to deserve such a fate. For though she'd known him barely a day, she already knew that there was no one else she'd rather trust with her life than Conor Quinn.

4

CONOR CIRCLED the block once just to make sure the house wasn't being watched. He didn't expect any surveillance at the landlady's place, though it never hurt to be certain. But he wanted the chance to check out Olivia's flat as well. He noticed a nondescript sedan with tinted windows nearby and made a note to call Danny and have him check it out.

He parked Dylan's Mustang a block away, then kept to the shadows of the houses. He took one last look over his shoulder before he climbed the front steps and rang the bell. Like so many other homes on St. Botolph Street, the spacious redbrick townhouse, once inhabited by a single family, was now divided into several apartments.

The lace curtain over the window fluttered and then the door flew open. He found himself face-to-face with an elderly woman, her gray hair askew and her faded housedress wrinkled. "It's about time," she muttered.

"Are you Mrs. Callahan?"

The woman nodded, her thin lips pursed.

"I'm here to pick up Tommy," Conor said.

She motioned him inside, then slammed the front door behind him. They were both crammed into a tiny little foyer and he pressed himself back against the wall as she moved around him, her ample body brushing up against his. "I'm damn glad to be rid of him," she said. "He's nothin' but trouble. Stays up all night long, sleeps all day, never stops eating. And the noise is about driving me to drink."

Olivia must have been in a desperate state to leave her son with such a harridan, Conor mused. He was glad that he'd be responsible for reuniting mother and son. And though protecting the two of them would be more work, at least there'd be a buffer between them, a reason to keep from touching her at every whim. "Where is he?" he asked, holding his arms up above his head to avoid touching the woman.

"He's on the bed in my bedroom."

"I'd appreciate it if you'd gather his things. I don't have much time."

Mrs. Callahan muttered a curse. "I should make you get him. He's got a wicked temper, that one. He'll scratch your eyes out." She sniffed disdainfully, gave Conor the once-over, then opened the inside door. "Wait here," she ordered.

As Conor waited, he peered out the lace curtains onto the street, puzzling over her words. He'd rather not give the neighbors anything to talk about, he mused. If he could get the kid to his car without being seen, then all the better.

A few moments later, he heard shouting from inside the house, then an ungodly howl that sounded more like an animal than a human being. He reached for the doorknob, but the door swung open in front of him. Mrs. Callahan shoved a cardboard box into his arms. "Good riddance," she said and moved to shut the door in his face.

Conor jammed his foot against the bottom of the door. "Wait a second. Where's Tommy?"

"He's in the box," the landlady said.

"In the box?" Conor carefully set the box on the hardwood floor, then peered beneath one of the flaps. A low growl emanated from the interior, and before he could pull his hand away, a paw snaked out and scratched him. Conor gasped, shaking his hand with the pain. "Tommy is a cat?"

"Yeah," Mrs. Callahan said. "What'd you think he was, one of them fancy French poodles?"

Conor didn't care to illuminate the old lady on his expectations. Right now he was having enough trouble keeping his temper in check. Of all the scheming, low-down, ridiculous— He ground his teeth, reserving his anger for the confrontation he planned to have with Olivia Farrell. "Does he have things? I mean, cat toys, food, stuff like that?"

"It's all in the box." She nodded, then smiled disdainfully. "Just don't touch his tail or you'll be scraping pieces of your hand off the ceiling." With that, she shut the door, leaving Conor cramped inside the little foyer with just a thin layer of cardboard separating his manhood from a spitting and hissing hellcat. He turned and opened the door, then hefted the box up into his arms. "You're going to pay for this, Olivia Farrell," he muttered.

As he walked down the sidewalk with Tommy the cat, the animal made a valiant attempt at escape. Though Conor was tempted to open the top of the box himself, after all the trouble he'd gone through to get the cat, he sure as hell wasn't going to let him go. After all, the cat was evidence. He was proof that Olivia Farrell had deliberately lied to him, had sent him on a fool's errand, and had put his life in danger in the process.

One of Keenan's men could have recognized him and taken a shot. Or he could be followed back to the motel where Keenan would take care of Olivia as well. Conor checked the street again as he put the box on the passenger seat of the Mustang. Then he jogged around to the other side of the car and hopped in.

He continued to watch his rearview mirror for signs of a tail and made a series of illogical turns through the South End neighborhood until he was certain he wasn't being followed. Then he headed for the interstate, his mind carefully reviewing the conversation he was about to have with Olivia.

Though he wanted to rail at her, to scold her until he extracted both a confession and an apology, Conor was secretly relieved. She didn't have a child. And without a child, there'd be nothing standing between them. He hadn't been sure what to think when she first mentioned Tommy, only that he felt an unbidden flicker of envy that her heart might belong to someone else.

Why feel envy, though? He'd tried to convince himself that his feelings for her were purely professional. After all, protecting people was what he did best. From the time he was a kid, he'd taken more than his share of responsibility. Still, he couldn't ignore the attraction between them, the sudden impulses to touch her and kiss her.

Hell, he'd heard about cops falling for the women they were assigned to protect and he'd always thought a guy had to be crazy to risk his career for a woman. But now he knew how it happened. She was just so frightened and needy, and his immediate instinct was to protect and to soothe. And sometimes nothing showed concern better than a kiss or a gentle caress.

Conor drew a sharp breath. He knew the rules, and the penalties for getting involved with a witness. If anyone found out, it could be the end of his career. He'd be back to walking a beat or, worse, be off the force altogether. And all for the pleasures of a woman! His father's warnings rang in his mind. The only thing that could bring down a Mighty Quinn was a woman. "So just keep your damn distance," he muttered.

As he drove south toward Quincy, he couldn't help but wonder if Olivia Farrell was worth the risk. The surge of desire he felt when he touched her, or the warm sensation of her lips on his, always seemed to thwart his common sense. Maybe it was because she was different from the girls he usually dated, girls he met in his father's pub, girls determined to tame a Quinn. Olivia was sophisticated and refined, elegant, the kind of woman who seemed...unattainable.

There'd been only one other woman in his life that had eluded his grasp. He'd been devastated when his mother had walked out, yet he still held her up as a paragon of womanhood. She was a lot like Olivia—beautiful, delicate, poised. Even though they'd been poor, she'd always set a proper table and taken special pains with her appearance and made sure her sons combed their hair before leaving the house.

As he had watched his parents' marriage fall apart

before his eyes, Conor wondered why Fiona McClain had married Seamus Quinn in the first place. They were like caviar and sardines, from the same place yet worlds apart. His mind drifted back to memories of happier times. But laced within those images were thoughts of Olivia. This time, he didn't brush them aside. Instead, like the rain pelting against the windshield, he let them wash over him. From now on that would be all he'd allow himself when it came to Olivia—an occasional impure thought.

By the time he pulled off the highway near Quincy, all the anger and resentment had faded. He stopped at a red light just a few miles from the motel, his mind focusing on Olivia. But the soft swish of the wipers was interrupted by a sudden flurry of noise. Conor glanced in the rearview mirror in time to see a shadow pass behind him. His first instinct was to duck, waiting for the sound of gunfire. But then he realized the ruckus wasn't coming from outside the car, but from inside!

He glanced over at the box on the front seat. The top was open and it was empty. "Damn," he muttered. It was like a cyclone had been let loose. Fur swirled in the air as Tommy raced around in circles, leaping over the front seat, bouncing off the back window, tearing across the dashboard, and whizzing past Conor's head. Conor tried to grab him, but the cat was too fast and his claws too sharp. He nicked Conor's chin and cheek on one lap around the interior and got him in the hand on another.

"All right!" Conor shouted. "I've had enough of this!" He yanked the steering wheel to the right and pulled over to the curb, ready to face the devil. Either he caught the cat and resumed control of the situation—or he turned the car keys over to Tommy. "I'm not handing the pink slip to this car over to a damn cat."

On Tommy's next pass, Conor gritted his teeth and grabbed at the blurry ball of fur. He caught hold of a leg and wrestled the cat back into the box, but not before suffering another round of injuries. "I should have just opened the window," he muttered as he threw the car back into gear, keeping an eye on the box.

By the time he pulled into the parking lot of the Happy Patriot Motor Lodge, he was bleeding from most of his wounds. But his pride had suffered the most. Hell, he'd brought down career criminals, ruthless men who wouldn't think twice before putting a bullet through his heart, and had come away without a scratch. It was embarrassing to be bested by a cat.

Conor grabbed the box from the front seat, then stalked toward the door. "She'd better be grateful," he muttered. "She'd better be damn grateful." He'd be satisfied with nothing less than a kiss—a long kiss, deep and wet. Brendan appeared out of the shadows and gave him a wave.

"Where's the kid?" he asked. He squinted in the low light. "And what happened to you?"

"There was no kid." Conor reached up to his cheek and came away with blood.

Brendan's eyes went wide. "You mean they got to him?"

Conor smiled and shook his head. "Tommy is a cat." He held out the box. "Take a peek. He's a fine little beast."

Brendan stuck a finger under the cardboard flap and was rewarded with a nasty howl and a vicious scratch. "Geez, what'd you do to the poor thing?"

"What did I do to him? Look what he did to me!"

With a slow chuckle, Brendan patted Conor on the back. "First a beautiful woman and then a cat. I knew when you finally fell, Con, you'd fall hard. Good luck to you. I expect you'll need it."

Conor stood in the rain for a long moment as he watched Brendan stride off into the darkness. Then he drew a deep breath and fished the room key out of his pocket. "Hold your temper, boyo," he muttered. "And watch your tongue. You have another ten days with this woman and you'd best make it easy on yourself."

When he entered the room, he found it empty. Fear stabbed at his gut, sapping the breath from his lungs. He tossed the box on the bed, ignoring the protests from inside. Had Keenan somehow gotten past Brendan? Or had Olivia slipped out without being noticed? He checked the window, but then heard the sound of the shower running.

With a soft oath, Conor crossed to the bathroom door and pressed his ear against the scarred paint. At first, he was tempted to open the door and make sure she was all right. But then he heard Olivia singing and he decided to bide his time until she emerged on her own.

He sat down on the bed next to the box to wait. Inside the cardboard cage he heard a low growl and then silence. Conor patted the top of the box. "Let's you and me get something straight," he murmured. "I'm the one in charge here. Either you listen to me or you'll be eating fish guts out of a Dumpster down by the water-front." He paused. "Are we clear?" He turned and looked through a small seam in the cardboard. An orange nose appeared and he was tempted to give it a poke. But he'd learned to be wary of both Tommy the cat and his mistress.

A few minutes later, Olivia emerged from the bathroom, a towel draped over her head, covering her eyes. Another towel was wrapped around her slender body and tucked between her breasts. Conor held his breath, not sure what to do. Propriety would dictate that he announce his presence, before she accidentally tossed aside both towels. Or maybe he should just make a quick exit and come in all over again. Or he could just turn and face the wall and—

The time to make a decision passed as soon as she wrapped the second towel around her damp hair and threw her head back. When she saw him sitting on the end of the bed, her eyes went wide. He waited, wondering just how offended she'd be. After all, she was naked under the towel and their relationship didn't really stretch that far—at least not yet. He slowly stood, his gaze never wavering from hers.

But instead of the expected indignation, relief suffused her flushed face. She let out a tiny scream, then launched herself at him, wrapping her arms around his neck and hugging him fiercely. At first, Conor wasn't sure what to do. And then he did the only thing he could think of doing. He wrapped his arms around Olivia Farrell's waist and he kissed her.

SHE'D BEEN SO overcome by her relief, Olivia didn't bother to consider the consequences of kissing Conor

Quinn. Throwing herself into his arms seemed like the most natural thing in the world. He was alive, he'd come back safe, and any guilt she had over sending him after her cat could now be forgotten.

Olivia wasn't sure who ended the kiss, although neither one of them seemed very anxious to pull away. But when she finally looked up into his eyes, she found them clouded with desire. Her gaze flitted over his handsome face and she noticed a trickle of blood on his cheek.

"You're wounded," she said, reaching up to touch him.

Conor grabbed her hand and gently drew it away. "It's nothing." He bent closer, as if to kiss her again, but Olivia wriggled out of his arms, her concern for his injuries taking precedence over her desire to feel his mouth on hers.

"Sit," she said, pushing him down on the edge of the bed. Olivia hurried to the bathroom and returned with a damp washcloth. She knelt on the bed next to him and examined his injuries. This served her right! She'd sent him off to retrieve her cat and he'd been grazed by a bullet. He could have been killed and all just to satisfy a silly whim, to give her a sense of control in this game they were playing. "I'm so sorry," she murmured. "I was selfish. I knew you thought Tommy was a child. Since you left, I've been feeling so guilty. I never meant for this to happen. Was it Keenan?"

"Not exactly," Conor said, his gazed fixed on her mouth as she tended to his wounds.

"Then one of his men?"

"No," Conor replied. "It was...your cat."

Olivia sat back on her heels. "Tommy did this to you?"

"Yes. And if you ever repeat that story, I'll fit you for a pair of cement overshoes and toss you in the Boston harbor myself."

Her eyes went wide then she saw the teasing glint in his eyes. "Do you forgive me?"

Conor shrugged. "You should have told me Tommy was your cat. I could have been better prepared. As it was, he tore up the leather upholstery in Dylan's '68 Mustang. I think he might have barfed on the floor. And I breathed in so much fur I should be coughing up a furball in an hour or two." Conor gave her a reluctant smile, then took the washcloth from her hand. "If you plan to let that cat out of the box, you'd better keep him away from me."

With a giggle, she scrambled over the bed to the box and called a soft "kitty-kitty." A "meow" sounded from inside the box and Olivia pulled back the flaps. Like a shot, a huge orange tabby leapt out of the box and onto the bed. She scooped him up in her arms and pressed her face into his fur, surprised at how happy she was to see him. "Were you a bad boy for Uncle Conor?" she cooed.

"I should charge him with assault on a police officer," he muttered.

Olivia set the cat down, then gave him a long scratch on the tummy before she turned back to Conor. A shiver skittered down her spine as she caught him staring. She didn't have to worry about his anger anymore, but there was something much more dangerous pulsing between them. She grabbed the washcloth from his hand and then she rummaged through her purse and found a small bottle of astringent she kept in her makeup bag.

"I expected you to take my head off," Olivia said as she poured a bit of the astringent on the washcloth.

"Believe me, I considered it."

He winced as she dabbed the astringent on his cheek. Olivia leaned closer and blew on his cheek to cool the sting. "There," she murmured. "That's better."

Conor slowly turned to face her. Their gazes locked and, for a long moment, Olivia couldn't breathe. She was suddenly aware that she was dressed only in a towel...a very thin towel. And that towel could be dispensed with by a mere flick of Conor's finger between her breasts. Another shiver skittered over her skin, raising goose bumps, and her eyes fell to his lips, hard and chiseled.

Her gaze was like a silent invitation and he accepted. He bent forward and touched his lips to hers. But this was the first time he'd kissed her merely to kiss her. Until now, their actions had been driven by impulse. This kiss was slow and measured and deliberate and Conor took his time with her, tasting and teasing until she tentatively opened for him.

As her lips parted, any attempt at resistance dissolved. Olivia knew it wasn't right, at least not by the policeman's handbook or her own set of relationship rules. He was a cop and she was a witness. They'd only known each other a few days. And although the kiss wouldn't cost her any more than breathless desire, it could cost Conor Quinn his job.

But she couldn't think of that now. Conor slowly pushed her back onto the bed, his mouth drifting down to the curve of her neck and tracing a warm path to her shoulder. Olivia closed her eyes and sighed, the sensations his mouth created sending tingles to her fingertips and toes.

It had been so long since a man had touched her that she couldn't bear to put an end to it. Nor could she deny the attraction she felt for Conor. Maybe it was a typical reaction, the vulnerable witness and the protective cop. It was almost a cliché, but then clichés always had a basis in reality—and her need was definitely real.

Conor was unlike any man she'd ever known and, in a secret corner of her soul, she wanted to know him more intimately. He was brave and volatile, funny and vulnerable, silent and strong, all qualities that had become pieces of a fascinating puzzle. What made this man tick? What piqued his desire? What was beneath that steely exterior? A man with such passion for his job must have other passions as intense. They'd spend the next ten days together and Olivia knew it would be impossible to deny her curiosity—or her desire.

"Why are you so soft?" he murmured, his lips pressed against her collarbone.

She furrowed her fingers through his hair as he moved to a spot just above her breast. "Why are you so tough?"

He glanced up at her and she saw it in his eyes, as if the sound of her voice had triggered a realization of what they were about to do. His jaw tightened and then he cursed softly and rolled off of her. Levering up, Conor swung his legs off the side of the bed. "You should probably get dressed," he muttered.

The regret was thick in his voice. But was it for what they'd already done or for what they couldn't do? Olivia readjusted the towel then sat up beside him, trying to maintain her composure. The towel suddenly seemed too small and too thin. "I guess we probably shouldn't do that again," she said, forcing a smile.

Conor shook his head. "It wouldn't be recommended. It's against almost every department rule."

"And if there weren't any rules?" she asked.

"I'm a cop and I deal with facts, not hypotheticals," he replied, the hard edge returning to his voice. He rose and then rubbed his hands together. "Why don't I go find us something to eat. You can finish...whatever it is you have to finish."

Olivia nodded, then hurried to the bathroom, anxious to escape his dark mood. She closed the door behind her, then leaned back against it. Her pulse still hadn't slowed and, though she wore only damp terry cloth, a flush had warmed her skin until it prickled with embarrassment. She turned and stared into the mirror, then sighed.

What stroke of luck—or misfortune—was responsible for all this? Why had she chosen to go into business with Kevin Ford? And why had she walked into the office at that very moment that her partner was meeting with Red Keenan? And why did the detective assigned to protect her have to be Conor Quinn?

"You used to be a lucky girl," Olivia said to her reflection. "Now you're plagued with misfortune."

She tossed aside the towel and gathered her clothes from the floor. But she was loathe to put them back on again. She'd been wearing the same clothes since they'd run out of the cottage on Cape Cod, a pair of jeans, a sweater, a camisole and silk panties. "I don't even have a change of underwear."

Olivia pulled on the jeans without underwear, then slipped into the camisole and the sweater. After the Tommy incident, she wasn't sure how much credibility she had with Conor. A sob story about clean underwear probably wouldn't go over very well.

She combed her damp hair and considered the best tactic to use, then remembered Tommy. He'd need food and litter and a litter box, maybe a few cat toys. A visit to the nearest discount store would take care of that, along with fresh clothes, underwear and a whole list of luxury items for her, like toothpaste and hand lotion and deodorant.

Olivia slowly opened the bathroom door, but the sound of Conor's voice stopped her. At first she thought he might be talking to Tommy. Then she wondered if one of his brothers had stopped by. But as she continued to listen, she realized he was on the phone with his station house.

"She's fine," he said. "What the hell happened to the officer at the cottage on the Cape? He was supposed to be watching the road and then he was gone." Conor paused. "He went for coffee and donuts? Listen, I want Carlyle or Sampson assigned to this case. In fact, send both of them. And don't go through regular channels; I still think Keenan might have someone inside the department." He paused again. "I can't. No, it won't work. It's...difficult. She's developed feelings for me. Yeah. You know how that goes. I just can't deal with her. All right. A half hour. Good."

Olivia slowly closed the door then sat down on the edge of the tub. He was leaving her to someone else? Just like that? She bit her bottom lip as a tremor of apprehension rocked her body. She trusted Conor. He was the only one who could protect her from Red Keenan. And she didn't want him to leave!

She fought the urge to walk out of the bathroom and tell him exactly what she thought of him! But then his words ran through her mind.

She's developed feelings...won't work...can't deal with her.

"He can't deal with me?" Olivia groaned softly. She'd thought that everything that happened between them had come from a mutual desire. Had she misread him? Was he only tolerating her until he could pass her off to one of his colleagues? Oh, God, how humiliating. She glanced around the bathroom, her gaze falling on a small window above the shower.

"I've got to get out of here," she murmured. "I just can't face him." But the window looked too small to crawl through. Maybe if she just locked herself in the bathroom until the other cops came, then she wouldn't have to talk to him again. But she didn't want to wait. All she could think about right now was escape!

CONOR STARED at the bathroom door, then glanced at his watch. She'd been in there for over fifteen minutes, long enough for him to run across the road to the convenience store and grab them a couple of sandwiches and a bag of cat litter. How long did it take to get dressed and fix her hair? Had he grown up with women in the house, he'd probably know the answer to that question. All he really knew now was that fifteen minutes should be enough.

He stood and crossed the room to the bathroom, then rapped his knuckles on the door. "Olivia? What's going on in there? Are you almost finished? I've got us something to eat." He listened carefully, but there were no sounds coming from inside the bathroom. Conor tried the door and found it locked. "Olivia, open the door." He knocked again, an uneasy feeling growing in his gut. "Damn it, Olivia, open the door or I'll break it down."

The threat was met with no reply. Conor cursed softly, then stepped away from the door. "If you're in there, you'd better step back." One swift kick right below the knob was all it took to splinter the cheap wood and to send the door crashing open. He hurried inside, expecting to find Olivia cowering in the bathtub. But instead he found a long pair of legs and a shapely backside hanging from a small window above the tub.

"What the hell are you doing?" he asked. "You can't get out that window—it's too small." He grabbed for her feet to pull her back inside, but she kicked at him, the heel of her shoe catching him in the nose.

"Leave me alone," she shouted, her voice muffled from the other side of the window.

Conor rubbed his nose. He'd had his share of bumps and bruises on the job, but this case was killing him!

"You'll never get through there," he said. "You're stuck."

"Don't you think I know that?" she called.

"Then just keep still and I'll pull you out." This time he grabbed her legs firmly enough so he wouldn't get kicked again. "Raise your arms over your head." She did as she was told, and with one good pull, she fell back into the bathroom—and into his arms.

They both tumbled to the floor in a tangle of limbs. Then she scrambled away from him, brushing her hair out of her eyes and tugging her sweater down from where it had bunched beneath her breasts. Conor sighed and leaned back against the wall. "What were you thinking?"

"Obviously, I was thinking I was a lot smaller than I really was," she shot back. "Remind me to lay off the French fries."

"Where did you plan to go?"

"Shopping," she muttered.

"Shopping?"

"Yes! If you must know, I needed some clean underwear. We ran out of that cottage on Cape Cod so fast that I didn't have time to grab my things. I've been wearing the same underwear for two days."

"Someone is out to kill you and you're worried about clean underwear?" he asked.

Olivia nodded, refusing to meet his gaze, her jaw set stubbornly, her arms crossed beneath her breasts.

Conor groaned inwardly. This was just another thing he didn't understand about women. This obsession with underwear. All the lace and the silk and the pretty colors. Underwear was underwear. No one saw it so what was the big deal? "Why didn't you just ask?"

"Because you don't care what I want or what I need."

"I don't care? Who risked life and limb to get your damn cat?"

She turned to face him, a defiant glint in her eyes. "If you really cared, then why are you leaving me? Why did you call for another cop to come and stay with me?"

Conor paused. So she'd overheard his phone conversation, and she'd obviously overheard the lies he'd told. Suddenly her reasons for climbing out the window became much clearer. He'd hurt her feelings, embarrassed her so completely that she couldn't stand to be in the same room with him. "I'm sorry. It's just that—"

"I know. I make it difficult for you. You can't deal with me. You made it sound like I was throwing myself at you. I thought the attraction was mutual."

He raked his hand through his hair, then slowly shook his head. "It was," he murmured. "It is. That's why I have to leave."

She turned, kneeling on the floor beside him, her expression anxious. "But what if I promise not to kiss you anymore? Would you stay then?"

"It's not you, Olivia," Conor said, reaching out to touch her cheek with his fingertips. "It's me. I can't promise that I won't kiss you again—or touch you. And if I can't promise that, then I'm not a very good choice to guard you. I need to be able to keep my head on the job or we're both at risk."

"But I trust you," Olivia said. "I don't want anyone else."

"The two guys they're sending are good guys. I know them both and I wouldn't let them stay with you if I wasn't sure they'd keep you safe. But I want you to promise me that you won't go climbing out of any windows or sending them after any more pets."

Olivia's gaze dropped to her lap. She studied her fingers for a long moment, then drew a ragged breath. "I don't want you to go," she repeated.

Conor hooked his finger beneath her chin and forced her eyes to meet his. The vulnerability had returned to her eyes and he fought the urge to kiss her again, to replace her sadness with passion. "Promise me?"

Reluctantly, she nodded. But Conor couldn't leave it at that. He gave in to the impulse and leaned toward her to brush a soft kiss on her lips. One last kiss. What could it hurt? he mused. But if he thought it would be enough, he was sorely mistaken. The moment her lips opened beneath his, he was lost in the warmth of her mouth. A low groan rumbled in his throat as he pulled her into his arms.

The taste of her was like a drug, so addictive that he'd risk it all to experience it just once more. Women had always been a "take it or leave it" kind of thing for him. He'd never felt the kind of obsessive attraction he had for Olivia, when every thought was consumed with the question of when he might kiss her next and how far that kiss might go. His brain clouded with the fresh scent of her hair and the warm sensations of her tongue teasing his.

It took all his willpower to draw away. He stared

down into her beautiful face and watched her eyes flutter open. "I want you to know that I lied on the phone. Kissing you isn't difficult. It's not kissing you that's hard."

A tremulous smile curved her lips. But her smile faded instantly as a knock sounded on the door of their room. She sent Conor a desperate look and he responded with a smile. "You'll be all right. I promise."

Conor stood, then reached out and helped Olivia to her feet. He moved to the door, Olivia's hand still tucked in his. He wanted to hang on to her for as long as he could. Later tonight, when he was alone in his apartment, staring at the ceiling above his bed, he'd want to remember how delicate her fingers felt and how sweet her voice sounded. He'd want to remember every second he had spent with her.

He carefully pulled back the curtain and saw Don Carlyle standing outside. Then he led Olivia to the bed where Tommy had curled up on one of the pillows. "Wait here," he said. "I'll just be a minute." Reluctantly, she let go of his hand and watched him walk to the door.

Conor stepped outside and closed the door behind him. He nodded a greeting to Carlyle. "What's the plan?"

"We've got a place for her over in Framingham. Sampson is waiting in the car." Carlyle cocked his head toward the door. "So what's her problem? She have a thing for cops or is she just one of those women who's happy with anything that wears pants?"

The anger was so instant and so intense that Conor didn't think before he acted. In one swift movement, he brought his arm up and shoved Carlyle against the door, keeping him pinned there. Conor moved to within an inch of Carlyle's face, then spoke in a low, even tone. "You make one move toward her, even look at her sideways, and I'll reach down your throat and turn you inside out. Got it?"

Carlyle frowned. "Yeah. I got it. Geez, Quinn, what the hell is wrong with you? You're the one who wanted out."

"Just remember what I said." Conor stepped back and Carlyle rubbed his chest. "She's a lady. Treat her like one."

Conor reached out and opened the door and Carlyle followed him inside. Olivia was in the same spot that he'd left her, perched on the edge of the bed, looking sad and vulnerable, hugging Tommy tightly to her chest. He crossed the room and gently took her arm. "Detective Carlyle is going to take you somewhere safe. If you need anything—" Conor smiled and leaned closer "—including underwear, you just ask. All right?"

He grabbed her coat from the bed, then held it out as she slipped into it. Then she gave Tommy a kiss and dropped him in the cardboard box. Carlyle looked at the box, then at Conor. "A cat? We can't take a cat."

Olivia's eyes went wide. "But I—"

"I'll take him," Conor said. "He can stay with me and you can pick him up after the trial." Though he hated the cat, he knew returning Tommy to his owner would give him one more chance to see Olivia, after all this was over and she was no longer a witness and he was no longer the cop assigned to protect her. A few weeks with Tommy the Terror was a small price to pay.

"You'd do that for me?" she asked.

Conor reached down and picked up the box. "Sure. By the time you come for him, we'll be old friends."

Olivia pushed up on her toes and gave him a quick kiss on the cheek. "Thank you," she murmured. Then she grabbed her purse and walked to the door. Conor followed her, taking one last look around before stepping outside behind her and Carlyle, the box tucked under his arm.

The next thing he knew, the wood from the door splintered next to his head. He looked out into the parking lot and saw another muzzle flash and the plate-glass window of the motel room shattered. Holding tight to the box, he shoved Olivia aside, both of them falling onto the walkway in front of Dylan's Mustang. "Stay here," he said, shoving the box into her arms. "And keep your head down."

Conor pulled his gun and peered around the side of the car. Carlyle was crouched beneath a rusted Pontiac, returning fire. From another spot in the parking lot, Sampson had pulled his gun and was taking aim. Conor crawled back to Olivia, then grabbed the box. "We're going to get in the car," he said. "Take the cat out of the box and hold on to him. Tuck him inside your jacket. We've got to do this quickly. Just stay low."

Olivia did as she was told and they both crawled around to the passenger side. He opened the door and she got in, then Conor scrambled around the front of the car. But the driver's side was in the line of fire and he knew he'd be taking a chance. Drawing a deep breath, he checked the clip in his gun, then shouted to Carlyle for cover fire.

He'd almost made it into the car when he felt a searing heat in his side, like someone had shoved a red hot poker between his ribs. The pain took his breath away and brought a wave of nausea.

Don't lose it now, his brain screamed. *Just get her out of here.*

Wincing with the pain, he yanked his door shut and shoved the key in the ignition. The engine roared to life and he threw it into reverse and backed out, pushing Olivia down in the seat with his right arm. Thankfully, Carlyle and Sampson kept Keenan's men pinned down. They managed to target the tires of the black sedan parked near the entrance to the parking lot so there would be no way for the gunmen to give chase.

When they were well out of range, Conor glanced over at Olivia. Her eyes were closed and her lips moved silently, as if she were praying. Tommy stared up at him with luminous eyes, content to stay clutched in Olivia's arms.

"We're good," he said.

Olivia gradually straightened in her seat, but didn't loosen her hold on her cat. "How did they find us?" she asked.

"Someone in the department," he replied. He turned and gave her an encouraging smile. "I guess we're on our own now." Another wave of nausea rolled over him and, for a moment, Conor had to fight to stay conscious. After nearly getting killed, the last thing he wanted was to run the car off the road. He pulled over onto the next side street and parked the car, then pressed his hand to his side. In the dim light from a streetlamp near the car, he saw the blood covering his fingers.

"I think you better drive," Conor murmured, suddenly exhausted by the effort that it took to move. He was going into shock and he wasn't sure how much longer he'd be able to keep his eyes open.

"Me? But why?"

"Just slide over," he ordered, pushing open the car door and stepping outside. It took every ounce of his effort to walk around the front of the car without keeling over. His legs felt like rubber and he was suddenly shivering for no reason. When he got back inside the car, he closed his eyes and focused on getting through a spasm of pain.

"Where are we going?" she asked.

"We need to get back to Hull," Conor replied, his voice tight. "To Brendan and *The Mighty Quinn*. Can you remember how to get there?"

Olivia nodded. "I think so. Are you all right? You look like you're going to be sick."

"I'm fine," he said through gritted teeth. "Just get us there." She reached for the ignition and Conor closed his eyes, confident that she'd get them back to the boat, back to safety. He felt himself growing tired and his eyes fluttered shut. But no matter how hard he tried to open them, the effort was too much. Blackness engulfed him and he finally lost his grip on consciousness.

5

OLIVIA BIT her bottom lip as she turned the ignition, sending up a silent prayer she wouldn't do anything stupid, like hit a parked car or run a red light. But when she reached for the gearshift between the seats, she realized prayers wouldn't do any good. A driving instructor might. "There's no *pernundul*," she murmured. No *P*, no *R*, no *N* or *D*. The car had a manual transmission and she'd never driven a stick shift before.

"I can't do this," she said. She glanced over at Conor. His head was tipped back and his eyes were closed. She knew he'd been working hard, but this was no time to take a nap! Olivia reached over and shook his arm. His hand fell between the seats, wet and sticky. She swallowed hard. Blood. "Conor? Conor, are you all right?"

Panic rose in her mouth like bile as Olivia shook him. He opened his eyes halfway and at first didn't seem to recognize her. "Are we there?"

Olivia leaned over and frantically examined his arm, then pulled his leather jacket open and found the source of the blood. All along his left rib cage, his shirt was seeped through. She felt faint and took a moment to draw a deep breath. "Oh, no, oh, no." She reached for the gearshift and studied the little diagram on the knob, then pushed in the clutch. "Oh, no, no." She knew the basics of a standard transmission, but she'd have to learn the finer points on the fly. "Hang on," she said. "Just don't die on me. Don't you dare die. I'm going to get you to a hospital."

"No," he muttered. "No hospital. Just get to Brendan. He'll know what to do."

She jammed the car into first, the gears grinding, then slowly let out the clutch. The car jerked and shuddered, but to her relief it started forward. By the time she'd circled the block, she had managed to try three of the four gears without stalling the engine. Olivia glanced both ways before pulling out on the highway, afraid to stop for fear she wouldn't get started again.

As she drove, she tried to contain a tremor that shook her body. "Stay calm," she murmured, searching the road for signs pointing to a hospital or for a pay phone to call an ambulance. She didn't want to obey his orders! He'd been shot protecting her and now it was *her* responsibility to save *his* life. "I'm going to call an ambulance," she said. "Give me your cell phone."

His hand shot out and clutched her wrist. "No," Conor insisted. "Do as I say."

"But the boat is at least ten minutes away. You could die before then."

"I'm not going to die," he replied. "I promise." He reached up and stroked her hair, the movement causing him to groan with the pain. "I'm not going anywhere."

Olivia glanced over at him, overwhelmed with concern and torn by indecision. "All right," she said.

"We'll go to the boat as long as you keep talking. If you pass out, I'm stopping to call an ambulance. Deal?"

"Deal," he murmured, his hand flopping back to his side.

She drew a ragged breath. "Fine. So what should we talk about? Let's talk about you. Tell me about your family. Tell me about Brendan and Dylan."

He moaned softly as he shifted in his seat. "Why do you want to know about them?"

"Just tell me," Olivia insisted. "Or tell me about your parents. Or your childhood in Ireland. Tell me where you were born. Just talk so I know you're still alive."

"I was born in a stone cottage that overlooked Bantry Bay," Conor began. "On the south coast in County Cork. My da was a fisherman. And my ma was...well, she was beautiful."

"When did you come to America?" Olivia asked, her mind jumping ahead, thinking of questions to keep him talking yet not really listening to the answers. She recognized the turn to Hull and said another quick prayer. They were only a few miles away. Now her only worry was finding the boat.

"She died," Conor continued.

Olivia glanced over at him. "What? Who died?"

"Or my da says she died. I don't think she did, because I would have known. But if she didn't die, then why didn't she come back?"

Olivia frowned. He was talking but he wasn't making much sense. "You don't know if your mother is alive or dead?"

"She went away when I was seven. One day she was there and then she was gone. Da wouldn't talk about it.

Later, he told us she died in a car wreck. But he was angry and I think he said that because he wanted us to forget her." Conor sighed and for a long moment he was silent.

Olivia thought he'd lost consciousness, but when she looked over at him his eyes were still open. "I never forgot her. The others did, but I didn't. I can still see her." He tipped his head her way. "She was pretty...like you. Only she had dark hair and yours is like spun gold."

His compliment was so simple and plainspoken that Olivia felt tears push at the corners of her eyes, tears of concern and affection and frustration. She was frightened, and usually when she felt that way, Conor made her feel safe. The thought that he might not be there to keep her safe tomorrow caused an ache to grow in her heart.

She turned back to the road and forced herself to concentrate. To her relief, she found *The Mighty Quinn* on the first pass along the waterfront. She slammed on the brakes and the car skidded to a stop on the street. Reaching a hand out, she placed her palm on Conor's cheek. "We're here," she said. "Can you walk?"

He nodded and she hopped out and ran around to Conor's side. She pulled, then dragged him to his feet, urging him to put one foot in front of the other and walk with her. Conor draped his arm around her shoulders and she bore most of his weight. He was still lucid, moving and talking, and Olivia hoped that she'd done the right thing bringing him here.

"What the—"

Olivia looked up to see Brendan coming toward

them from the boat. "Help him," she said. "I think he's been shot."

Brendan grabbed Conor's other arm and wrapped it around his neck and, in a few moments, they were helping Conor into the cabin and onto a long narrow berth.

"It hurts like hell," Conor murmured, "but I don't think it hit anything vital."

Olivia stepped away as Brendan tended to his brother, the impact of what had happened suddenly hitting her full force. Her hands began to tremble and her breath came in quick gasps. Tears scalded the corners of her eyes. Brendan tugged off Conor's jacket and she moaned along with him, feeling his pain.

"God, Con, there's an awful lot of blood." Brendan turned to Olivia and pointed to the far side of the galley. "There's a first aid kit on the bulkhead. Grab that and a few clean towels."

Olivia did as she was told. Brendan flipped the kit open and rummaged around until he found a small bottle of alcohol. "Shouldn't we call an ambulance?" she asked. He doused one of the towels with it then pressed it against Conor's side.

Her question was met by a loud string of colorful curses. Startled, Olivia stepped back. Brendan chuckled and glanced over his shoulder at her. "It's the sting from the alcohol." He turned back to Conor. "It looks like a flesh wound, not too deep, just a lot of blood. I've got a buddy here in town who's a doctor. I'm going to call him."

"It's a gunshot wound. He'll have to report it and they'll know where we are," Con said. "You stitch it up, like you stitched up Da's arm that time when he got caught in the line."

"Con, we were four hundred miles out to sea and I used an old needle and some fishing line. I'll explain to my friend that you're a cop. And he'll report it tomorrow morning. By that time we'll be gone." Brendan grabbed a cell phone from the table and dialed a number, then spoke in soft, urgent tones to his friend.

At the same time, Conor looked over at Olivia and gave her a weak smile. She walked over to the berth and knelt down on the floor, then took his hand. "I was so scared," she murmured. "I still am."

"We'll be fine," he said, pulling her hand to his lips. "You did good."

She sat on the floor next to him, holding his hand, until the doctor arrived. Then Brendan drew her out of the cabin up to the deck. Olivia was glad for the fresh air. She was weak and dizzy, and if she had to watch Conor's pain for a moment longer, she was sure she'd faint.

They stood at the rail and stared out at the dark harbor, listening to the clank of rigging and the soft lap of the water against the hull. "You've had quite a night," Brendan said.

"I thought I had a pretty exciting life before this," Olivia murmured. "I travelled, I went to fancy parties, I took nice vacations. That was nothing compared to spending time with your brother."

Brendan wrapped an arm around her shoulders. "Thanks," he said.

She glanced up at him. "For what?"

"For saving his life. For caring about him."

"That's not hard to do," she said, a tiny smile quirking her lips. "He's a good man. Maybe the best man I've ever known."

"But sometimes he makes it hard to like him. He keeps his distance, and when anyone gets too close, he retreats."

"He told me about your mother," she said.

Brendan blinked in surprise. "Conor talked about Ma?"

Olivia stretched her arms out over the rail and stared at her hands. "I don't think he realized what he was talking about. He was just talking to stay awake."

"I think that's the reason Conor keeps to himself," he said. "When she left, he was the one who took the brunt of it. He was a kid raising five other kids. I don't think he ever wants to be deserted like that again, so he closes himself off to the possibilities and turns his energy into making everyone feel safe." Brendan sighed. "He still thinks Ma is alive."

"Do you think she is?"

Brendan shrugged. "I don't know. When we were little, Con said he would go to find her when he was old enough. Maybe that's why he became a cop. Or maybe it was because he needed to take care of everyone else's troubles. He's kind of codependent that way. But I don't think he's ever looked for Ma."

"Why not?"

"I think he was afraid of what he might find. He was happier believing she was alive somewhere, alive and living a good life." Brendan pushed back from the rail. "I'll go see how things are going. Can I get you anything? Coffee, tea? A shot of whiskey?"

Olivia smiled and shook her head. When she was alone, she walked along the deck to the bow of the boat. The shadows from the quay cast the bow in darkness and she sank down, her strength finally giving out and her emotions taking over. A sob tore from her throat and she hugged her knees to her chest and let the tears fall.

They fell for the life that she once had, calm and orderly, and for all her hopes for the future. They fell for her anger at her business partner and at Red Keenan. But mostly, they fell for Conor, for the boy he was and the man he'd become. A man who'd risked his life for her, a man she was fast falling in love with. And a man who might never return that love.

"Olivia?"

She raised her head and quickly wiped away the tears, then stumbled to her feet. Brendan was waiting for her at the entrance to the main cabin. "He's going to be fine. The doctor stitched him up. The bullet just grazed him."

A fresh round of tears flooded her eyes and Brendan drew her into his arms. "Come on. It's all right now. The doc and I moved him into my cabin where he'll be more comfortable. And I brought your cat in from the car." He leaned back and gave her a smile. "Why don't you go see him. I have to hide the car before someone recognizes it. Then I'll run and get you both something to eat. Do you want anything special?"

"Little Friskies in the can," she said. "Tuna flavor. And some kitty litter. For Tommy."

Brendan chuckled. "I'll get you a burger." He nodded toward the cabin. "It's the companionway that leads to the bow of the boat."

Olivia wiped her cheeks again and ran her fingers through her hair, hoping that she looked at least presentable. Why she bothered to worry about her appearance, she wasn't sure. Conor had certainly seen her looking worse. But she wanted to be strong for him and looking like she was falling apart didn't cut it.

When she reached the forward cabin, she knocked on the door, then stepped inside. The soft glow from an oil lamp washed the cabin in flickering shadows. Conor lay on the bed, bare-chested, eyes closed, a bandage taped to his rib cage. His jeans had been cast aside and the waistband of his boxers was visible where the bedsheet was twisted around his waist. Tommy was sitting silently on the end of the bed, keeping guard over the man that had saved them both. Olivia distractedly scratched the cat's ears as she stared at Conor, her gaze transfixed by the planes and angles of his face.

Awake, he always had a hard edge to him, his gaze intense and his jaw tight. But as he slept, she saw a side of him revealed rarely, only in a fleeting glimpse when he smiled. Olivia tiptoed over to the bed and knelt down beside him. His hair fell over his forehead, just touching the dark slashes of his eyebrows.

She looked closer, surprised that she'd never noticed how long and thick his lashes were. Beautiful, she mused. Not a word one would usually associate with a man like Conor Quinn. Desire welled up inside of her, unbidden but undeniable. She'd always been so careful with men, but with Conor all her resolve seemed to crumble with just one touch.

He was arrogant yet affectionate, dangerous yet vulnerable, contrasts that she found irresistibly intriguing. She'd never felt such an instant connection with a man before. With a hesitant hand, she reached out and tenderly brushed the hair out of his eyes. Her breath stilled and she bent over him and placed a gentle kiss on his lips.

Conor's eyelids fluttered and he awoke.

FOR A MOMENT, he thought he might be dreaming. The light from the oil lamp shimmered around her head, like a halo. And then his vision cleared and he found himself looking at an angel come to earth. Conor smiled sleepily. "Hi," he murmured.

Olivia leaned forward and gazed into his eyes. "How do you feel?"

"Like hell," he said. "But the doctor says I'll be fine. A little sore for a while. And I'm going to have to give up my Olympic dreams in the javelin and shotput."

She giggled and the sound brought a small measure of relief. Brendan had told him that Olivia had been close to tears when they'd arrived. It was nice to see her smile again. Just looking at her exquisite beauty was the best medicine he could have.

"Brendan went to get us something to eat. Are you hungry?"

He pushed up on his elbow, pain shooting through his side. "I'm starved," he muttered through clenched teeth.

"Here," Olivia said. "Let me help you." She placed her arm around his shoulders and helped him sit. His face nuzzled into her chest as she moved him and he groaned inwardly, trying hard to ignore visions of the warm flesh beneath her sweater. When she had stacked a few pillows behind his back, Conor closed his eyes and leaned back, trying to banish the heat that had shot to his groin. At least he knew the bullet hadn't injured that part of his anatomy.

"What are we going to do now?" Olivia asked, sitting down on the edge of the berth.

"Bren called my little brother Liam. They're going to help Brendan take the boat up to Salem. My brothers Sean and Brian will meet us there with another car. After that, we're going to get lost until the trial."

"Don't you think you should call your boss and tell him we're okay?"

"I'm not playing by the rules anymore. I did, and it almost got us both killed. If they thought I was a rogue cop before, they haven't seen anything yet."

"All right," Olivia said. "Whatever you think is best."

A soft knock sounded at the door and Olivia walked over and opened it. Brendan stood outside with two paper bags. He handed them to Olivia. "I've got cat food. Why don't you send Tommy out and I'll feed him." He looked over to Conor. "Liam's here. We're going to be casting off in about a half hour."

Olivia set the bags on the bed, then picked up the cat and shooed him out the door. When she and Conor were alone again, she carefully opened the Styrofoam containers. "We have a hamburger...a hamburger... and—ah, something different—a cheeseburger."

"My brother has very basic tastes when it comes to food," Conor said.

Olivia plucked a French fry from the bag and held it out in front of Conor's mouth. He grabbed it with his teeth and quickly devoured it. It was the best French fry he'd ever eaten and Conor wondered whether that had less to do with the chef and more to do with his dinner companion.

After they finished, Olivia cleaned up the wrappers and the soda cans, then took them out to the galley. When she returned, she stood in the doorway of the forward cabin, her hands clutched in front of her. "I guess I should let you get some rest. I'll just find a spot for myself in—"

"No," Conor said. "Stay here. I'll sleep better knowing you're close by."

She gave the twin-size berth a long look and Conor could tell exactly what she was thinking. In order for both of them to sleep in it, they'd have to practically wrap their bodies around each other. "I'll stay until you fall asleep," she said, moving to sit on the edge of the berth.

He nodded, then closed his eyes. "Tell me a story," he said. "When we were kids, my brothers and I always had a story before bed."

"About what?"

"Fairies and gnomes and elves."

"Well, I know the story of Thumbelina," she said.

"Is that an Irish fairy?"

"No, I think it's just a fairy tale."

"I suppose that will have to do. Tell me, then."

Olivia drew a deep breath and began to speak.

Though her story seemed to be an odd amalgam of several different Disney movies, Conor really didn't care. He just wanted to listen to her voice, to reassure himself that she was still safe. As she launched into a subplot that had something to do with a cricket, he reached out and took her hand between his, distractedly toying with her fingers.

His touch caused her to hesitate for a moment, as if the warmth from his fingers had swept the words from her head. But then the story continued, through his gentle exploration of the soft skin on the inside of her wrist and inner arm, past the point where he gently pulled her down next to him on the bed, and beyond the moment when he tucked her body against his. It was only then that he could finally close his eyes and sleep, when his arms were wrapped around her waist and the sweet curve of her backside was tucked in his lap.

Conor drifted in and out of sleep, the painkillers the doctor had given him causing fitful dreams. He remembered hearing the engines start and then the gentle motion of the boat as it cut through the water. Olivia slept soundly, her body soft and warm in his arms, her breathing slow and even. Now that they were on the water, he was certain he could keep her safe. And though he'd always hated *The Mighty Quinn*, he had to appreciate the old boat for taking them out of danger.

Salem was fifteen miles across Massachusetts Bay and a busy harbor town. The boat could get in and out without much notice. Though Conor wanted to put his plans all together in his head, his brain was too fuzzy to concentrate for long. Instead, he nuzzled his face into the curve of Olivia's neck and closed his eyes again.

He wasn't sure how long he slept, but the next thing he remembered was the boat bumping up against the dock. Olivia rolled slightly with the motion and he grabbed her tight to keep her from falling off the berth. She stiffened in his arms and he knew she had awakened. When she turned onto her back and glanced up at him, it was with uncomprehending eyes.

"We're just tying up," he whispered, her face so close to his that he could feel her breath on his skin.

She didn't say anything, just stared into his eyes. And then Conor bent closer and touched his lips to hers. He really hadn't expected her to respond, but when she did, he deepened the kiss, lost in the enticing taste of her mouth.

Everything about her was too much to resist and he didn't want to make the effort anymore. He'd been alone for so long and, for the first time in his life, he'd found someone who could make him forget all of the barriers he'd built around his heart. She touched a spot, deep inside of him, that he hadn't even known existed. And when he kissed her, he didn't have to wonder whether his kiss was making promises he didn't want to keep. For now, Olivia was his and that was all that mattered.

Her pale hair fanned out on the pillow and Conor ran his fingers through it, liquid and silken to his touch. She moaned softly and wrapped her arms around his neck, then teased at his bottom lip with her tongue. He sensed that her need for him was as acute as his was for her. And though he could spend the entire night just kissing her, the urge to explore her perfect body was just as overwhelming.

Somewhere in the recesses of his mind, a little voice—his cop voice—told him that spending the night in the same bed broke all the rules. And making love to her could end his career. "Why do you taste so damn good?" he murmured. "I want to stop but I can't."

She sighed softly, her fingers skimming over his face. "There are rules," Olivia whispered, "against this..." Her tongue teased at his nipple. She trailed lower, nipping and biting, and driving him mad with need. "And against this..." she said, her fingers splaying across his belly, causing a flood of heat to rush to his lap.

He'd already decided that when it came to this case, the rules didn't apply anymore. Someone in the department had nearly gotten them both killed. The police were supposed to be the good guys. Those were the rules. If they couldn't follow them, then he wouldn't either. "From now on, we make up our own rules," he said. "And rule number one is that there will be no more rules."

A playful smile quirked the corners of her mouth. "I like that rule."

He laughed softly, then captured her mouth with his again. He'd never have guessed that behind her cool, sophisticated facade lurked an uninhibited temptress. Conor turned to pull her nearer, but the shift in his weight caused a sharp pain in his side, deep enough to steal his breath. He cursed softly. "This is not going to work," he said. "I can barely move."

"Then don't," Olivia said, straddling his hips and

bracing her hands on either side of his head. "Rule number two. You must stay perfectly still."

Her hair created a curtain around them and she dropped a kiss on his mouth and then another and another, dancing away when he tried to take more. When she straightened, Conor reached out and slipped his fingers beneath the hem of her sweater. He spanned her slender waist with his hands and reveled in the beauty and delicacy of her body.

She was made for his hands, every curve a perfect fit against his palms. Though he'd never touched her this way before, it was as if he knew her by instinct. Yet that didn't stop him from wanting to explore and memorize every inch of her skin.

With other women, it had been all about him and his needs, the undeniable rush toward satisfaction. Maybe it was the way he and Olivia had begun, his focus on protecting her. Suddenly, he wanted to make her ache for him the way he ached for her. He needed to see the desire grow in her eyes and feel it in her hands, until nothing could stop them from the inevitable.

Conor slid his hands along her rib cage until he found the soft curves beneath her breasts. The silky fabric of her camisole beneath his palms enhanced every warm inch of her flesh. As if taking a cue from him, Olivia reached for the buttons of her sweater and slowly undid them. When she was finished, he reached up and skimmed the sweater off her shoulders and down along her arms.

He'd chided her for her underwear obsession at the motel, but now he understood. The lace edging of her camisole offered a tempting view of the cleft between her breasts and the silk clung to her body like a second skin, outlining the peaks of her nipples.

With her eyes fixed on his, her gaze challenging him to make her stop, Olivia reached for the hem of her camisole and pulled it up over her head, then shook her hair until it tumbled around her shoulders. Conor's breath caught in his throat. She was the most beautiful thing he'd ever seen, her skin luminous in the soft light. He knew at that moment that he wanted her, more than anything he'd ever wanted in his life. But he schooled his need and promised himself that he'd go slow.

His reached up and cupped a breast in his palm, teasing at her nipple with his thumb. What bit of luck had brought her into his life? What had he done to deserve her? Whatever it was, Conor wasn't about to question his good fortune. He'd simply enjoy it while it lasted. Never in a million years could he hope that Olivia would want a future with him.

But he did know one thing. He was fast falling in love with Olivia Farrell, with her beautiful eyes and her incredible body, with her stubbornness and with her vulnerability. With the way she made him shiver with anticipation. He slipped his hand beneath the hair at the nape of her neck and slowly drew her back to him, covering her mouth with his. The blood rushed hot through his veins and his pain was forgotten as he rolled her over beneath him.

His mouth ached to taste her, his fingers craved the feel of her skin. Slowly, Conor explored her body with both, gently arousing her desire then letting it ebb. He wanted this to last as long as it possibly could, for

Conor wasn't sure they'd have this chance again. But the more he touched her, the more irresistible she became.

Conor wasn't sure at what moment they reached the point of no return. Perhaps it was when she stood beside the berth and slipped out of her jeans. Or maybe it was when he cast aside his boxers. But by the time she'd retrieved a condom from Brendan's bedside table and slipped it over his hard shaft, he was certain he was lost.

She straddled his hips, then slowly sank down, taking all of him, to the hilt. For a long moment, Olivia didn't move, her eyes closed, her head tipped back. Conor's jaw went tight as the sight of her alone almost brought him to his peak and he realized that he'd relinquished all control. She was the seducer and he was the seduced.

As if caught in a dream, Olivia started to move above him, rocking slowly at first and then increasing her rhythm. It took all his willpower to wait, to tease and touch, to grasp her waist and slow her movement, until she was ready to join him. He waited for the signs, the soft sighs, the shallow gasps of breath that marked each thrust, the subtle tensing of her body.

And when she was ready, he touched her once more, at the spot where they were joined. She stilled, and then he felt her tighten around him in an exquisite spasm. She murmured his name, once, and then again, and then Conor let himself go, arching into her.

Waves of sensation shattered them both, leaving them breathless, a sheen of perspiration the only thing separating skin from skin. And when it was over and they'd both drifted back from the edges of passion, she curled up in his arms and closed her eyes.

He knew this time it had been different. They'd shared something that he'd never shared with a woman before, an intimacy so deep and stirring that it caused his heart to beat more strongly and his mind to sharpen. She'd broken through a barrier and touched his heart and, in that instant, he knew what it would be like to love a woman, so deeply that it defied reason.

Conor closed his eyes and tried to sleep, but he was afraid that when he woke up, she'd have slipped away in the night, like a dream. He turned his face into her hair and inhaled the scent, then ran his hand along her thigh. She was real and the pleasure they'd shared was real.

He didn't want to let her go. Not now. Not ever.

OLIVIA WOKE sometime in the early morning hours, confused at first by her surroundings. Then she heard Conor's soft, even breathing and the tiny edge of fear dissolved. She was safe, wrapped in his arms. For a long time, she watched his naked chest rising and falling, slowly, steadily. The lines of tension that had bracketed his mouth and eyes were finally gone and she gently smoothed her fingers over his face as if to erase the last traces of pain.

A wave of emotion washed over her. How had she grown so attached to this man in such a short time? They'd known each other less than seventy-two hours, yet she felt as if she'd already spent a lifetime with him. Circumstances had thrown them together, given them a common enemy and forced a trust that might have taken years to build, but in reality had taken no more than a day.

He had a beautiful body, lean and hard, smooth skin covering carved muscle. His broad shoulders and chest tapered to a flat belly and narrow hips. It had been so long since she'd been intimate with a man that Olivia had forgotten what the sight of the male form could do to her resolve.

Still, making love after such a short time wasn't really her habit with men. But Conor was different. She trusted him with her life, why not trust him with her body? Though she'd only known him for a few days, that had been enough for her to see that he was a good man, an honorable man. And no matter what the future held for them, she was sure she'd never regret her choice.

But then again, she didn't really have a choice. The first time Conor had touched her she'd been lost. What had happened between them was inevitable and so were the feelings that came with it. She tried to convince herself that she could separate sex from love—and maybe she could have with another man. But with Conor, her feelings were so intense, so undeniable, that she couldn't tell where love began and sex left off.

For the next ten days, they'd live together in a world of their own making. And when it was time to go back to the real world, she'd have to deal with the consequences. Until then, she'd cherish every touch and every kiss.

Olivia drew a deep breath, then let it out slowly. The scent of coffee drifted through the chill morning air and she squinted in the low morning light to read her watch. "Six a.m.," she murmured. Though she wanted to wake Conor with languid kisses and tempting caresses, to rediscover the passion they'd shared the night before, she knew he needed his rest.

She slowly rolled out of bed, careful not to disturb him. Piece by piece, she plucked her clothes off the floor and got dressed. She slipped out of the forward cabin and into the bathroom—or the "head" as Brendan had called it. After brushing her teeth with her fingers and raking her hands through her tangled hair, she ventured out to the main cabin, craving a hot cup of coffee.

Olivia expected to find Brendan up and about, but she walked into an entire cabinful of men. They all had gathered around the table, each of them with a steaming mug of coffee. Even Tommy was there, perched on a shelf and accepting small treats of table scraps. She paused, then smoothed her hands over her sweater. "Good morning," she murmured, wondering if the events of last night were evident in her appearance.

Brendan pushed up from the table and smiled warmly. "Hey, Olivia. How's the patient doing?"

She glanced back over her shoulder. "He's still sleeping," she replied. "I—I think he's feeling...fine." She felt a warm blush creep up her cheeks. He was better than just fine, she mused. He was incredibly gentle and intensely passionate. And after a night in bed with him, she felt exhausted and exhilarated at the same time.

"I don't think you know everyone here. You met Dylan a few nights ago." He pointed to the youngest man at the table. "This is Liam. And across from him are Sean and Brian."

Olivia frowned. All of Conor's brothers resembled each other with their dark hair and their unusual hazel eyes. But Sean and Brian looked almost identical. "Twins?" she asked.

They nodded in unison. Olivia had been an only child but had always wondered about the bonds between siblings. They must care for Conor very much to leap to his aid so quickly. Somehow, she knew she'd come to no harm as long as the Quinn brothers were standing behind her.

"Come on," Brendan said. "Have some coffee. Liam brought donuts and muffins. I hope you don't mind— I fed your cat."

Olivia found a place between the twins. Tommy watched her with wide eyes. She'd never considered her cat very sociable, but he seemed right at home among all these men. She noticed the empty tuna can on the table. Either Conor's brothers had unusual tastes in breakfast food, or they'd been spoiling her cat rotten.

Brendan set a mug of coffee in front of her and she picked it up, grateful for the warmth. The brothers all stared at her, as if she were some kind of bizarre lab specimen and she shifted uneasily, not sure what to say.

"So, what do you do?" Dylan inquired. "I mean, when you and Conor aren't dodging bullets?"

His teasing tone was so like Conor's that Olivia immediately felt a level of comfort that she shouldn't have felt among strangers. "I sell antiques. I have a small shop over on Charles Street." She took a sip of her coffee. "That's how this all started. My partner was laundering money for a mobster."

"And how is it, living twenty-four seven with our Conor?" Sean asked.

"It's nice," Olivia said.

Brian chuckled. "Nice. Con?"

"He's not bad. He takes good care of me. Sometimes he gets a little impatient, but that's only because he's concerned for my safety. And I—"

"What are you boys up to?"

They all turned to find Conor standing at the far end of the cabin. He'd managed to pull on a pair of jeans but hadn't bothered with the top button. His hair was tousled and the bandage was stark white against his rib cage.

"What are you doing out of bed?" Olivia asked. She scrambled from her place at the table and crossed the cabin. Conor winced as she draped his arm over her shoulders and walked with him back to the table. He didn't bother to sit and Olivia could see what it was costing him. It was as if he didn't want to show any sign of weakness.

"So tell me what you have for me," Conor said, glancing at each one of his brothers.

"Brian got you a car," Dylan said. "It's parked at the end of the dock. It's wicked ugly, but it runs. I brought you some fresh clothes. They're in the trunk."

"Here," Brendan said. "You can take my cell phone. I'm not sure if they can trace the calls on your phone, but it's better to be safe for now."

"We should stay here for a little while longer," Olivia suggested. "You need to rest."

"No," Conor said, not bothering to look her way. "We'll leave in a half hour."

"But—"

Conor turned to look at her, his gaze unyielding. "This is not up for debate," he said. "We'll do it my way."

Olivia bristled at the tone of his voice, so different from that of the night before, and she felt a flush of embarrassment creep up her cheeks. He turned and started back to the forward cabin. Olivia glanced around the table. "He should rest," she murmured. "He was shot."

Brendan shrugged, then sent her a sympathetic smile. "Con does things his own way."

Olivia spun on her heel and followed after Conor. When she reached the forward cabin, she stepped inside and closed the door behind them. Conor stood beside the berth, trying to slip into his shirt.

"Why do we have to leave?" she asked, holding onto the shirt as he twisted into it. "We're safe here. And you need to rest." He refused to answer her, focused on his shoulder holster. "What is this?" she demanded. "Are you determined to kill yourself just to show your brothers what a tough guy you are?"

He glanced up at her. "Don't think because of what happened last night I'm going to stop doing my job," he murmured. "I'm paid to protect you and if that means we move, then we move."

Stunned by his indifferent tone, Olivia wasn't sure what to say. Had she imagined what they'd shared last night? Was she naive to believe that it changed things between them? With a soft curse, she grabbed her purse, her shoes and her jacket, then yanked open the cabin door. "Forgive me," she muttered. "I didn't realize that what happened last night was all part of the job."

Olivia walked out into the main cabin and didn't bother turning around when he called her name. Maybe this was all for the better. They'd had a little fun and now it was time to get back to business. She was a witness and he was a cop and she'd do well not to forget that in the future.

But Olivia knew in her heart that it would take her a very long time to forget her night with Conor Quinn—if she could forget it at all.

6

"WHAT THE HELL are you doing?"

Conor stepped out of the forward cabin only to find his two brothers blocking his way with broad shoulders and angry expressions. "What do you mean?"

"She's out there on deck and I think she's crying," Dylan said. "What did you do to her?"

"Nothing," Conor replied. "I'm just doing my job, that's all."

Dylan shook his head. "You seduced her, didn't you. You slept with a witness."

Conor cursed softly. "I did not—"

"Come on," Brendan said. "One look at that girl's face was all it took to know what went on in *my* cabin last night in *my* bed. She looked, as we say in the literary world, well bedded. And knowing your lack of preparedness when it comes to matters of the heart, I'm sure all I'd have to do is count the condoms in my bedside table to figure out how great the night really was."

Conor had never been one to open up his private life to family scrutiny. As far as his brothers were concerned, he didn't have a private life. "All right," he said. "So we...were intimate. Don't tell me you guys never lost control with a woman."

"Not me," Dylan said.

"Never," Brendan added.

"Well, someday you will," Conor warned, "and then you'll know what it feels like. I couldn't stop myself. It seemed—no, it *was* the right thing to do. I...care about her." He drew a ragged breath, then stepped around them to grab another cup of coffee. His side was beginning to ache again and perhaps the caffeine would dull the pain. "Da always warned us about women being the only thing that could bring a Quinn down. I have to tell you, last night, I didn't care. I wanted to be brought down. I wanted to forget about that stupid family curse."

"So what's your next move?" Dylan asked.

Conor was glad for the change of subject. Now that he'd admitted his weakness, he didn't want to dwell on it. But his reaction to the events of last night had carried into the morning. He wasn't sure what had happened between him and Olivia, beyond an incredible physical release. He only knew that it had changed something deep inside of him, opened a door that he'd always kept firmly locked.

"I called my partner," he said.

"I meant what's your next move with Olivia. If I were you, I'd apologize for every stupid thing I said. And then I'd thank my lucky stars that a woman like her wandered into my life."

"Well, I'm not you, Dylan," Conor murmured. He took a sip of his coffee. "Danny found us a place to stay."

"Can you trust him?" Brendan asked, concern coloring his tone.

Conor brushed him off with a shrug. "The kid transferred to the district three months ago. Even the most corrupt cop doesn't go bad that fast." He turned and leaned back against the rail. "His grandmother just moved to Florida and he's selling her condo for her. It's still furnished. He says we can stay there as long as we want."

"So you're going to play house with Olivia until the trial?" Dylan asked.

"I'm keeping her safe," Conor countered.

Brendan shook his head. "She's a nice lady, Con. I wouldn't want to see her get hurt any more than she already is—and I'm not talking about bullets here."

"Neither would I," Conor murmured as he ran his fingers through his hair. But then maybe he already had hurt her, simply by making love to her. Though their night together had been incredible, it was also a dangerous move. She'd come to depend on him, first for her safety and now for intimacy, and he wasn't sure that he could continue to give her what she needed.

Soon, they'd be free to go their separate ways. Would she be able to let go? And even more importantly, would he? "Right now everything is so unreal," he said. "Feelings are magnified because of the circumstances. She can't possibly know how she really feels. To her, I'm some big hero. Believe me, give her time. She'll figure out who I really am."

"And what if she does and she doesn't turn and run?" Dylan asked.

"Did you ever think she might be the one?" Brendan asked.

"Maybe," Conor said. "But I can't think about that

now. From now on, I have to concentrate on the job and nothing else."

Brendan stepped around him to the hatch, then climbed the stairs. "Just don't be such a hard ass, Con. Give her a chance."

Conor and Dylan followed him out and they found Olivia sitting on a locker, her hands clasped on her lap. She'd pulled her hair back into a ponytail and her fresh face was barely touched with makeup. Whether in the soft glow from an oil lamp or the bright morning sunshine, Conor thought she was the most beautiful woman he'd ever seen. An image of her flashed in his mind, her hair tumbling around her face, her body flushed with passion and his blood warmed in the chill morning air.

"I'm ready," she murmured as she stood.

Given the choice, he'd rather take her by the hand and lead her back into the cabin to kiss away the tension that had sprung up between them and spend the day lost in carnal pursuits. Hell, why not stay on the boat and just jump from harbor to harbor until it was time to go back. Brendan could take them down the coast to Martha's Vineyard or Nantucket. Or they could go farther south, looking for warmer weather.

Conor considered the notion, then cursed inwardly. Already she was making him question his decisions, put aside his responsibility as a cop for a few more adventures in the bedroom. If he wasn't careful, that would put them both at risk.

"I told Olivia I'd take care of Tommy for her," Brendan explained. "He seems to like it here and I could use the company. When things have settled down, she can come back and get him."

Olivia pushed up on her toes and gave Brendan a quick kiss on the cheek. "Thank you," she murmured.

It was only a kiss of gratitude, but Conor didn't like it. He knew Brendan all too well, knew his penchant for charming the ladies. While Brendan was smooth and disarming, Conor had always been lacking in social skills. He'd never developed the ability to sweet-talk a woman, to enthrall her with just a few well-chosen phrases. Women usually found him attractive for what he didn't say, rather than what he did.

"Yeah, thanks," Conor said, holding out his hand for Olivia. She said her goodbyes to Dylan, and Conor watched as his brother grabbed her around the waist and swung her up onto the dock. He jumped off after her, then held his hand out to Conor.

Conor ignored the offered aid, clenched his teeth, and swung up onto the dock himself, ignoring the sharp ache in his side. He'd only been up for an hour, but already the nagging pain was making him edgy. Hell, he was ready to bite his brothers' heads off for touching Olivia.

Brendan and Dylan accompanied them to the end of the dock. When they reached the car, Dylan tossed him the keys, then jogged around to the opposite side to gallantly open the door for Olivia. Before he closed it, he leaned inside and whispered something to Olivia. She giggled softly then gave him a wave goodbye.

Conor started the car and then pulled away from the dock. As they drove through town, neither one of them said a word. He considered apologizing for his curt words. He even thought about bringing up the subject of their night together, laying down some new ground rules. But he knew the chances of him saying something stupid were pretty high. Maybe if he just didn't mention it, they could go on as they had before.

As they headed away from the water toward the interstate, he risked a glance over at her, curious to know what Dylan had whispered, yet too stubborn to ask. Olivia's gaze was fixed on the road ahead and she clutched her fingers in her lap, as if sitting next to him made her uncomfortable.

Conor turned his eyes back to the road, then noticed a sign for a discount store on the right. He glanced over his shoulder, then pulled into the parking lot. Olivia sent him a questioning look. "Where are we going?"

He smiled. "You'll see."

He found a spot near the entrance, then hopped out of the car to open Olivia's door. But she had already stepped out by the time he got there. Conor took her hand, glad to have an excuse to touch her again, and led her through the front doors. He glanced at the store directory, grabbed a shopping cart, then pulled her along behind him.

When they reached the lingerie department he stopped. Then he reached into his pocket, pulled out his wallet and handed her a credit card. She looked down at it. "What's this for?"

"Underwear," he said. "On the Boston P.D. Go crazy. Buy as much as you want." A slow smile curled her lips and relief flooded his senses. He could still make her happy.

"Underwear?"

He nodded, his heart warming beneath the delight on her face. Her earlier anger was quickly forgotten. "Even though you're used to wearing designer clothes, discount is all I can offer for now," Conor said. But that didn't stop him from wanting to give her more. "Buy anything else you need."

With a cry of delight, she wrapped her arms around his neck and gave him a fierce hug. "Underwear," she said in the same tone that a woman might say "diamonds" or "pearls." Olivia stared up into his eyes for a long moment. He fought the crazy urge to kiss her, trying to ignore the perfect shape of her mouth and the way her lips glistened beneath the harsh store lighting. He put aside the vivid memories of all the kisses they'd shared already. But, in the end, he couldn't pass on the chance to steal just one more.

Conor bent his head and touched her lips with his, just barely a kiss, yet enough to satisfy his craving and reassure himself that he'd repaired any damage he'd caused to their relationship. Then Olivia turned and began to pick through the displays and racks. At first, Conor stood back, observing her selections. But when she disappeared into a fitting room, he wandered over to a bin of black underthings. He picked up a pair of panties, no more than two scraps of satin and a bit of lace, and studied them for a long moment.

"Can I help you?"

Conor spun around to find an owl-eyed saleslady looking at him through horn-rimmed glasses. He cleared his throat and quickly wadded the panties and shoved them into his jacket pocket. "No," he murmured. "I—I'm just waiting for someone."

"You aren't planning to steal those panties, are you?" she asked.

Startled, Conor laughed uneasily. Then he reached into the back pocket of his jeans and produced his badge. "I'm a cop," he said.

She peered at his badge, then back at his face. Conor shifted uneasily. What? Did she think he planned to wear the panties himself? He pulled the panties from his pocket just as Olivia emerged from the fitting room.

"I'm done here," she said, piling her selections into the cart. "Can we look for a few T-shirts and sweaters?"

"Sure," Conor murmured, surreptitiously tossing the black panties into the basket as well. Then he gave the saleslady a dry smile and turned back to Olivia. "Come on, let's go."

They wandered around the store, Olivia stopping in nearly every department to browse. When she got to the men's department, she pulled a couple of flannel shirts from a table, then tossed in three T-shirts. Though he didn't say anything before she moved on, Conor liked the idea of her choosing his clothes. It was a familiar, almost intimate, gesture that warmed him in the same way her touch did.

"Before we go, we need to get some medical supplies," Conor said after a half hour of shopping. Though he was loathe to put an end to her fun, his side was beginning to ache incessantly. "Bandages and alcohol and adhesive tape."

Olivia frowned, then moaned softly, her eyes going wide with concern. "I—I'm sorry. Oh, I forgot all about your wound. Let's go." She grabbed the cart and hurried down the aisle toward health and beauty. But as they passed the men's underwear department, Conor remembered he could use some extra boxer shorts. Maybe it was optimistic to believe Olivia might see his underwear again, but it paid to be prepared. He had no idea whether Dylan had thought to bring him clean underwear. Conor veered off and grabbed a few packages, then tossed them into the cart.

When they reached the checkout counter, Olivia picked the merchandise out of the basket and put it on the conveyor belt. But when she came to the black panties, she held them up, then glanced at Conor suspiciously. He forced a smile, then gave her a shrug. "How did those get in there?"

For a moment, he thought she might hand them to the checker to return to the shelf. But then she tossed the panties down next to the others, a tiny grin curling the corners of her mouth. Conor let out a tightly held breath, imagining how she'd look in black satin, imagining himself as he hooked a finger beneath that lace and tugged them down her legs.

As he walked out of the store carrying Olivia's bags, he considered the possibilities that their purchases held. And though he should have pushed the idea from his mind without a second thought, Conor couldn't help but wonder what their next night together might bring.

"IT'S A RETIREMENT COMPLEX," Olivia murmured, staring at the entrance to Waterbrook Manor. "'A complete residential community for active seniors'?" she read. "I don't think we're going to blend in here," she said.

"Maybe not," Conor said. "But then this is the last place Red Keenan would look. I doubt that the people here have any underworld connections. And it's rent-free. No one can track us."

But Olivia had learned to be suspicious of every situation. They were supposed to be safe at the Happy Patriot and Conor had gotten shot. They should have been safe on *The Mighty Quinn*, yet they'd stayed there only one night before running again. "Are you sure you can trust your partner? What if he tells someone where we are?"

"He won't," Conor said. "He may be green, but he's loyal." He put the car into gear and drove up the winding drive, past a group of seniors playing bocci ball and around a crowded putting green. The complex was huge, with four-unit condos set amidst tidy landscaping. They found the address, in a building set back from the road, and parked. But Conor waited before getting out.

"We need a story," he said.

"Like one with fairies and gnomes?" Olivia asked.

"No, a cover story. Something to tell people if they ask."

"We could say that we're renting the condo while Danny tries to sell it. Helping to make his grandmother a little extra pocket money."

"That's good," Conor said. "It makes us sympathetic." He paused. "And I think we should tell them we're married."

Olivia gasped. "What?"

"It only makes sense," Conor said. "There are bound to be people here who frown on premarital...well, you know...relations. An unmarried couple cohabitating. I just don't want to give them an excuse to gossip."

"All right," Olivia said, seeing the sense in his explanation. Besides, what harm could it do? Just because they said they were married didn't mean they had to continue the roles behind closed doors. "We'll tell them we're newlyweds. That we eloped last week."

"Eloped?"

She held up her hand and wiggled her fingers. "No rings."

"That's good," he said. "You're really getting the hang of this."

Olivia felt a small measure of pride at his compliment. At least she'd contributed a little something to the team. "I have a good teacher. Now how are we going to explain the lack of luggage?"

"We're having our things sent...from Seattle," he said. He reached in the back seat for their shopping bags. "That should take some time. And later we can tell them the moving van was in an accident and all our things were destroyed."

Olivia nodded. In truth, she was relieved they'd be sleeping in a decent place tonight. She imagined a long bath and a warm bed. She'd had precious little sleep over the past few days and, right now, all she wanted to do was crawl beneath a cozy blanket and drift off for a day or two. But as she contemplated the pleasures of hot water and a soft mattress, her mind spun a fantasy of both that included Conor.

Every time she thought of them alone, she thought of

them together—in the shower, in the bedroom, even on the kitchen counter. She couldn't help but wonder what the night might bring. A shiver of anticipation skittered up her spine.

Neither she nor Conor had mentioned the events of the night before. It was as if avoiding the subject might just turn it into a dream. Olivia had searched his eyes every chance she got, hoping to see some trace of the raw emotion that had swept them away. But the Conor she'd made love to was gone. In his place was the Conor that had only one purpose in mind—keeping her alive to testify.

An odd sensation gripped her stomach. Was that what last night was about? She'd been upset over the shooting. Had he made love to her because he cared, or because he wanted to make sure her worries were soothed? Disturbed by her doubts, she hopped out of the car before Conor could open the door for her. The condo was located on the upper level of the building and they climbed the outside stairs, then found the key where Danny Wright had hidden it.

As the door swung open, Olivia stepped inside, curious to see where they'd be spending the next nine days. The apartment was tiny but very tidy. A small living room was sparsely furnished with a sofa, an easy chair and a television set. In the center of the living room, a pair of plastic garbage bags sat on the rug. Olivia crossed the room and looked inside the first one, then smiled. "Our things from the beach house." She made a mental note to give Danny Wright a big hug.

To the left of the front door was a small dining area and a galley kitchen, stocked with utensils and pots and pans, enough for them to cook at home. And down a short hallway were a bedroom and a tiny bath.

"It's very nice," Olivia said as she wandered into the bedroom. She bounced on the edge of the bed. It didn't squeak. "Better than the Happy Patriot."

Conor turned away from the door, as if the sight of her and the bed made him uneasy. "We'll be safe here," he mumbled, "and that's all that counts."

They walked back to the kitchen just in time to hear a knock at the open door. An elderly woman took a step inside. "Hello," she said, eyeing them both warily.

"Hello," Conor replied.

"I'm sorry to interrupt, but I just wanted to check on Lila's apartment. This is where Lila Wright lives. Are you friends of Lila's? We all like to watch out for each other and Lila moved to Florida to live with her sister and—"

"I'm a friend of Lila's grandson," he explained. "Danny Wright? He's renting us the place until he sells it—you know, to help Lila out. My name is Conor. Conor Smith and this is Olivia Far—Olivia Smith. My wife." He glanced at Olivia. "She's my wife."

"We just got married," Olivia said brightly, stepping to Conor's side and looping her arm through his.

Conor quickly put his arm around her shoulders and pulled her a little closer. "We're very happily married," he said.

He felt Olivia's elbow in his ribs and he was glad she wasn't standing on the other side of him. "I think we'll be very happy here," she said, glancing around the condo.

The elderly woman sent them both a dubious look.

"You do understand that this is a seniors' complex," she said. "There's not much excitement around here, unless you count that fist fight that broke out at last week's pinochle tournament. Bert Blevins accused Harvey Denton of cheating and Harvey punched Bert in the nose and—"

"Well," Conor interrupted. "I've always been very mature for my age and so has Olivia. Besides, we really wanted someplace quiet. No loud music, no parties. We're very private people."

The woman glanced back and forth between the two of them, then finally nodded. "I live just across the stairway. My name is Sadie Lewis." She held out her hand and Olivia quickly reached for it. "Congratulations, my dear."

"Congratulations?" Olivia asked.

"On your marriage," she said. "You two look very happy."

"Oh, we are," Conor said. "Very happy." He gave Olivia another hug. "We are newlyweds, after all," he said, this time with more meaning.

Sadie got the message, then nodded knowingly. "I think I'll just leave you two alone. If there's anything you need, don't hesitate to ask. I'm right there." She pointed to the front door of her apartment, just twelve feet away from theirs.

"We won't," Conor said as he closed the door behind her. "Bye now."

As soon as the door was closed, Olivia hauled off and punched him in the shoulder. "Gee, why beat around the bush? Why not just say, me and the missus want to have sex now so we'd appreciate it if you'd leave?"

"I thought it was the quickest way to get rid of her. She seemed nosy and nosy people will hang around as long as you let them." Conor glanced down at her. "What? Are you embarrassed? We're just pretending."

Olivia turned away from him. But they weren't just pretending. They'd made love last night, or had he forgotten so soon? "No. I just don't want her thinking—"

"Thinking we're hot for each other?" Conor chuckled, as if the notion was preposterous.

Why was he trying so hard to forget what they'd shared? She bit her bottom lip, trying to keep from blurting out her feelings. She already knew that Conor wasn't the type to reveal his innermost thoughts. It would probably take major surgery to find out what was inside his heart.

"I need to change this bandage," he finally said, grabbing one of the bags from the discount store. "Why don't you make a grocery list and I'll go out and get some things for dinner?" With that, he strode down the hall, leaving Olivia to wonder whether she really had imagined their night together.

After a quick survey of the kitchen, she sat down at the dining table and began a grocery list on a scrap of paper from her purse. But by the time she'd finished with nine days' worth of provisions, Conor still hadn't emerged from the bathroom. Hesitantly, she pushed up from the table and walked down the hall. "Conor?" she said, rapping softly on the door. "Are you all right?"

"Yeah," he snapped from the other side of the door. Olivia heard a soft string of curses. "No."

She slowly pushed the door open to find him standing in the center of the bathroom, shirtless. He'd managed to get the bandage off but his attempts to replace it had been thwarted. Adhesive tape lay tangled on the floor and gauze pads cast aside. Cotton balls saturated with alcohol made Olivia's eyes sting.

"I need help," he muttered. "I can't reach around and get the tape on straight."

Olivia stared at him for a long moment. In the harsh light of the bathroom, he looked even more magnificent than he had on the boat. She could see every muscle in his back and torso, bunching and shifting beneath his skin as he turned to tend to his wound. Olivia wanted to run, certain that touching him would transform her into a babbling fool. But common sense told her that she owed it to him to help.

The bathroom was so tiny, she was forced to close the door in order to have enough room to work. She grabbed the tape from his hand, then pulled two gauze pads from the paper package. "Put your arm up," she murmured.

He did as he was told and Olivia got her first real look at his wound. She winced at the angry red slash in his side and the line of neat stitches that kept it closed. "It looks painful," she said.

"Actually, I was thinking that it wasn't so bad after all. I doused it with alcohol and smeared on some of that antibiotic salve the doctor gave me. It only hurts when I twist or reach."

She pressed the gauze over the wound, then put his

right hand on top of it. A length of tape secured it on top and Olivia tore off three more pieces and taped the bandage in place. "There," she murmured, slowly straightening.

In the cramped quarters they couldn't help but touch each other as they moved around. His body brushed against hers, her breasts pressed to his naked chest. And then, suddenly, his arms were around her waist and her fingers were splayed across his chest. Conor captured her mouth with his in a frantic kiss, his hands skimming along her hips, drawing her closer.

The kiss took her breath away, full of fierce longing and fully realized need. He'd kissed her for no reason at all, only that he'd wanted her at that very moment. All her worries about his motives dissolved and Olivia was certain of his desire. He wasn't playing a role to keep her happy, he wanted her, now more than ever. He had been affected by the passion they'd shared.

But just as she allowed herself to revel in the taste of him, he pulled away, as if ending the kiss quickly would make it seem like it never happened at all. "We shouldn't do that," he said, his jaw tight.

Olivia wrapped her arms around his neck and smiled. He could make a feeble attempt to deny her, but in the end, he couldn't resist. "Why not?"

Conor shook his head, then grabbed his shirt from the edge of the tub and struggled into it. "We just shouldn't. It complicates things."

"It doesn't have to," Olivia said. "What we share here is between us and no one else."

She saw the battle in his eyes, between common sense and carnal pleasures. But she'd spoken the truth.

If all they had was the next nine days, then she'd understand. The past three had been the most exciting days of her life and she couldn't regret a single minute, not if it brought her closer to Conor Quinn.

Conor dragged his gaze from hers. "I have to go," he said.

Olivia blinked in surprise. "Where?"

"I've got some things to do."

"I'll come with you," she said.

"You'll be safer here."

"Aren't you afraid I'm going to leave?" Olivia asked.

Conor thought about the suggestion for a moment, then shook his head. "You know the dangers out there, Olivia. If you really want to leave, I can't stop you. But I'd be damn angry if I came home and found out that I took a bullet for a woman who cared less for her life than I do."

With those words, he made it clear that to leave would be a betrayal he couldn't forgive. Olivia took a deep breath, then nodded. "I'll be here when you get back. You don't have to worry."

She stood in the bathroom and listened to his footsteps as they retreated down the hallway. For a few minutes there, she really believed she understood Conor Quinn. But then he threw up walls all around him, determined to keep her at a distance. Olivia couldn't blame him. After what she'd learned about his childhood, it was no wonder he was wary of women.

Still, she'd seen a vulnerable side of him and it gave her hope that, one day, Conor might want to love her. With a long sigh, Olivia sat down on the edge of the tub. "I should find myself a nice, normal guy," she murmured, her chin cupped in her hand.

But she didn't want normal. She wanted dangerous. And if the past few days had proved anything at all, it was that Olivia was beginning to thrive on danger.

THE OFFICER on duty recognized Conor the moment he walked in. But Conor had counted on the code between cops, a code that called for silence until questions were asked. He walked up to the desk at the Suffolk County Jail and pulled out his badge. But he didn't reach for the pen to sign in, bypassing the strict requirements called for when visiting a prisoner.

"Quinn," the officer nodded.

"Mullaney," Conor replied.

"Didn't expect you to turn up here," Mullaney murmured, leaning forward as he lowered his voice. He glanced over Quinn's shoulder. "I hear the D.A. and the brass are ready to can your ass. You kidnapped a witness."

"I'm just doing my job," Conor murmured. "I'm supposed to keep her alive until the trial. And it looks like someone in the department wants her dead."

Mullaney blinked in surprise, then nodded as if he sympathized with Conor's predicament. "I suppose I should be forgetting that I saw you tonight."

"And while you're at it, you can forget that you called Kevin Ford up to an interview room by mistake. And that I just happened to be in that interview room when he arrived."

"If they find out about this, your career will be over," Mullaney said.

"I'm still a cop and he's still one of the bad guys and, until he asks for his lawyer, we're just a couple of buddies chatting about a mutual acquaintance."

"If anyone asks, I never saw you. Just make sure no one else never saw you, too. Room seven."

He picked up the phone to call the guard on duty, then buzzed Conor in. He'd been to Suffolk hundreds of times before to interview suspects. He knew how to walk through the place without being recognized, how to avoid contact with anyone who looked like a lawyer. He stepped into the interview room and, a few moments later, a uniformed officer opened the door and let Kevin Ford enter.

Ford was dressed like all the other prisoners in a baggy jumpsuit. Yet he still seemed completely out of place. His pale face and horn-rimmed glasses gave him the look of a Harvard professor rather than the career criminals that populated the county jail. He walked into the room, hands cuffed in front of him, then sat down across from Conor.

Conor had developed the ability to read suspects, to know exactly what kind of people they were and what buttons to push to get them to talk. Kevin Ford was easy. He was a coward at heart, willing to do whatever it took to save his butt. The problem was Red Keenan was willing to do whatever it took to kill Ford's butt if he talked.

"I'm not saying anything without my lawyer. And I'm not going to testify against Keenan, so you might as well not waste my time."

"Yeah," Conor said. "I bet your social calendar is pretty full." He chuckled softly. "Nothing you say is going to leave this room. I'm officially not here and we're officially not talking."

"What do you want? Did Keenan send you?"

Conor tried to keep the surprise from his expression. "Keenan?" he asked. "I guess he's sent his cops around to talk to you already." Better to act like he knew exactly what Ford was talking about. "So did he send the guys in uniform or did he send his detectives?"

Ford didn't answer, but Conor could see it in his eyes. Someone from the department *had* talked to him, convinced him not to testify against Keenan, and that someone was a cop. "You don't have to answer that," Conor said. "If he'd sent the top guys, you'd be a lot more messed up."

That seemed to bother Ford, the look on his face shifting to one of fear. "You know what I don't get?" Conor continued. "How a guy like you, smooth, sophisticated, well-read, a guy with real manners, could hang Olivia Farrell out to dry? She didn't do anything to you except trust you. You were her friend. And now she's got Keenan's men shooting at her. She'll testify, and her testimony will probably put both you and Keenan away for a long time. But she'll spend the rest of her life looking over her shoulder."

Ford hung his head, his attention fixed on his folded hands. "I didn't mean to get her involved." He glanced up and, in that single moment, Conor saw the truth, all laid out in front of him. Kevin Ford was in love with Olivia Farrell!

"Why did you do it?" Conor asked, his jaw tight.

"Off the record."

"I bought the shop on Charles Street. The mortgage

was killing me, I made a few bad buys and suddenly I was on the verge of losing it all. I couldn't let her down, so when Keenan came to me, I took him up on his offer. At first it was just supposed to be a short-term deal. But then once I was in, I couldn't get out."

Conor almost felt sorry for the guy. Hell, he knew how Olivia could twist a man's heart a million different ways, and how Keenan could take advantage of any vulnerability. "You said a cop came to talk to you about Keenan?" Ford nodded. This was the break he needed, a way to extract Olivia from this mess and still send Keenan to prison. "What if I found a way for you to testify against Keenan, to put him in jail for the next twenty years?"

"I'm not going to testify," Ford insisted.

"What if you didn't have to do any time? I could make that happen," Conor said.

"My lawyer says I might not do any time anyway," Ford replied.

"Your lawyer is overly optimistic. Olivia's testimony will put you in jail. And I'd wager you're not the kind of guy who'll do well in prison. Even if it's only a few years, those years won't be kind."

Ford's shoulders slumped further. "Why do you care about me?" he asked.

"I don't care about you," Conor said. "I care about Olivia."

They exchanged a long look and Conor knew they understood each other perfectly. They'd both fallen for the same woman, both shared an instinct to protect her. "If you can guarantee that I'll stay out of jail, then I'll testify against Keenan."

Conor pushed to his feet. "Don't tell anyone about this, not even your lawyer. I'm going to send a detective to talk to you. His name is Danny Wright and he works for the good guys. He'll set this up for you. You can trust him."

Conor strode to the door, then hammered his fist on the window. The officer waiting outside unlocked the door and Conor stepped out. Anxious not to be seen, he hurried down the corridor and past the desk, not stopping to talk to anyone. When he got outside, he stood on the street, breathing deeply and running the plan through his mind.

Until that moment, staring into Ford's eyes, he hadn't recognized his feelings for Olivia, hadn't believed they could have a future together. But now he knew. He was in love with Olivia Farrell. He'd known her for three days and already he knew he wanted them to spend a lifetime together.

But it wasn't as easy as it all looked. Even if he wanted Olivia in his future, he didn't know if he even had a future to offer her. Hell, he wasn't sure how this would all turn out. Even if Ford made the deal, Conor was still facing some pretty serious accusations, so serious that they could cost him his job. And without a job, how could he possibly plan a future for them?

"Quinn!"

Conor spun around. Danny Wright was jogging down the sidewalk toward him. He waited for his partner, then pointed down the street where he'd parked his car.

"What are you doing here?" Danny asked, breathless.

"I was visiting Kevin Ford," Conor admitted.

Danny stopped short on the sidewalk and shook his head in disbelief. "You talked to Ford? Aw, man, this is bad. I don't mean to question your procedures, but everyone at the station is talking. First, you disappear with a witness—a beautiful, female witness—and now, you're sneaking around, talking to the perp."

Conor chuckled at Danny's police slang. "How'd you know I was here?"

"Mullaney called me at the station house. He told me to come down here and pick up my stuff. It took a while, but I figured that he meant you."

"Well, talk all you want," Conor said. "Because right now I'm not listening. I've got other things on my mind." Olivia. He had Olivia on his mind and all the things he had to do to make this work for them both.

Conor turned to Danny. "Keenan has a guy on the inside. That's how they keep getting to us. And Kevin Ford knows who he is. I told Ford you'd be visiting him. I want you to find out all you can, then take it to Internal Affairs. They'll offer Ford a deal in exchange for the dirty cops. And Olivia won't have to testify."

Danny frowned. "But what if—"

"Just do it," Conor said. "And watch your back."

Danny nodded, then Conor slapped him on the shoulder and smiled. "You're a damn good detective, Wright." A smile broke across his partner's face and Conor took that as his cue to leave. He grabbed the car door, pulled it open, then hopped inside. And as he drove off down the street, he let out a tightly held breath.

"This has to work," he murmured to himself. It was

the only way he could be sure that Olivia stayed safe for the rest of her life. And right now the only thing in the world he cared for—the only thing that made any difference in his life at all—was Olivia Farrell.

As for their future together, he'd have to think about that later. "One step at a time," he said softly.

7

SHE'D BEEN CAUGHT in the middle of a wonderful dream. Everything was so warm and comfortable, the sun, the water, like a little Jamaican vacation in her sleep. Olivia smiled and snuggled down beneath the quilt she'd pulled from the bed. The television glowed in the darkened living room, a travel show softly playing in the background.

For a long time, she drifted in and out of the dream, spinning images in her brain of her and Conor, lying on the sand, swimming naked in the ocean, making love in a hammock. After this was all over and she was safe again, maybe she'd ask him to take a little vacation. She had some money saved and she probably wouldn't have to worry about her business since there wouldn't be much left to worry about.

It would be fun, a chance to really get to know each other. She turned the notion around and around in her mind. But before she'd imagined the most perfect vacation with the perfect man, she heard the sound of the door opening. Olivia opened her eyes, then pushed up on her elbow and watched Conor slip into the condo. He'd been gone for most of the day and into the evening and, though she really hadn't worried about him, she was curious about what had occupied his time.

In truth, she was also a bit jealous that he could go

out and walk around without worrying about his safety and she was stuck inside for the entire day playing the responsible witness. So she'd made the best of the situation and spent a lazy hour in the bathtub. After that, she lounged around the condo, watching soap operas and painting her toenails.

"You're home," she murmured, running her fingers through her tangled hair.

Startled, Conor turned and peered into the dim living room. Then he shrugged out of his jacket, tossed it on a chair and slowly walked over to her. "Were you sleeping?" he asked.

Olivia smiled and stretched her arms over her head. "I've been a lazybones all day long. It felt good to finally relax. We've been kind of busy lately."

He sank down on the end of the sofa, far enough away from her that she couldn't give him the hug she wanted to. In truth, he didn't seem in a very huggable mood. He tipped his head back and stretched his legs out in front of him. "Yeah, we have. It takes a lot of energy to dodge those bullets."

Olivia scrambled to her knees, reminded again of his injury. She settled beside him. "How are you feeling? Does your side hurt?"

Conor winced as he shifted his weight. "It's not bad. Most times I don't notice it."

"Why don't you let me get you some dinner?" she said, crawling off the couch. She picked up his feet from the floor and swung them around. "You stretch out and rest. I'll let you know when dinner is ready."

He groaned, then rubbed his eyes. "I didn't get any groceries. I'm sorry. I had to take care of some police business and then I met Danny and I talked with him. Then I stopped over at Dylan's place. I just lost track of time."

He made to get up, but she gently pushed him back down. "We don't need groceries," she said. "We have neighbors. Sadie from across the stairs brought us a tuna noodle casserole and an apple pie. Louise from downstairs, who is married to a retired Navy man, brought us a taco casserole and a fruit salad. And Geraldine, who used to be a Rockette, brought us a little honeymoon basket with candles and champagne and some chocolate. There are cookies from Doris—she's so funny—and some fresh lemonade from Ruth Ann who looks a little like my landlady. And we're invited to join the canasta club on Tuesday, the bocci ball couples' tournament on Saturday, and the potluck supper on Sunday night."

"I see you've been as busy as I was," Conor murmured.

Olivia sighed. "We've lived here one day and I already know five of my neighbors. I've lived in my flat on St. Botolph Street for six years and I know two people—the woman who rents the downstairs apartment and my landlady who lives down the street."

"Don't get too used to it," Conor muttered. "We won't be staying forever."

His tone had an edge to it that she'd never heard, not even when he was ordering her around. She tried to read his mood. So often over the past few days, he'd let his guard down. It just surprised her when those barriers suddenly appeared again, in the tone of his voice or in an impatient sigh. She didn't need to be reminded that they'd only be together a finite time. She reminded herself of that same thing every day—every time she looked into his eyes or touched him, every time she remembered their time together on the boat.

But Olivia had already decided that she wouldn't think about the future, even if that future was only a week away. She wanted to live for the moment, to enjoy Conor while she had him, for she knew once his responsibility to her was through, he'd rebuild all those walls so he could walk out of her life.

"Why don't you put your feet back up," she said. "I'll get us some dinner and then we can have a quiet evening. No bullets flying, no car chases."

That brought a tiny smile to his lips. He stretched out on the sofa, not even bothering with his shoes and, in a few minutes, he'd fallen asleep. Olivia gently covered him with the quilt then wandered into the kitchen. She grabbed the tuna casserole from the refrigerator, then popped it into the oven.

As she searched a drawer for serving utensils, her mind wandered to Conor. She found herself pretending that he'd just come home from a long day at work, that she'd met him at the door with a kiss, that they were married and living a happy life together. She'd never imagined an ordinary life for herself. When she'd imagined marriage, it was always so much more exciting and urbane.

But then the excitement didn't really come from a fancy apartment or a glittering social life. It came from moments like these, moments when she could make Conor's life more comfortable, moments when she could walk in the other room and just touch him when she wanted to. Olivia smiled, then pushed up on her toes and retrieved two wineglasses from the top shelf in the kitchen cabinet. But halfway there, she froze.

A soft sigh slipped from her lips. What was she doing? All these silly fantasies, tropical vacations, quiet evenings after work? "He's a cop, you're a witness," she murmured. She'd have to remind herself of that more often. This wasn't a fairy tale romance with a happy ending, this was a few stolen days with a handsome cop who'd been assigned to protect her.

A half hour later, the tuna casserole was bubbling in the oven and she'd set the coffee table in the living room for an impromptu meal. She retrieved the champagne from the fridge, then lit the candles that Geraldine had tucked in the basket. It all looked perfect...romantic.

Olivia frowned. Was she being too presumptuous thinking that Conor might want to share a romantic evening with her? Whether she acknowledged it or not, this whole meal was a prelude to seduction. She'd secretly hoped that the candlelight and the champagne would lead to a few fleeting kisses. That those kisses would lead to a few more. That they'd end up passing the night in a passionate interlude in her bed.

She moaned softly, doubts assailing her. This was way too obvious. She had to play harder to get! Reaching out, she grabbed one of the candles. But the sharp movement caused the wax to drip onto the back of her hand and she bit her lip to keep from crying out. She dropped the burning candle and it tipped over on the table, landing on the pile of paper napkins that she'd set out.

In an instant, the napkins ignited. Olivia grabbed the champagne bottle and with fumbling fingers, tried to remove the cork. But before she could, the smoke alarm on the ceiling went off, a shriek loud enough to pierce her eardrums.

Conor bolted upright and reached for the gun in his shoulder holster, dazed and confused. He glanced around the room, then scrambled off the sofa when he saw the small fire on the coffee table. "What the—" He snatched the champagne bottle from her hand and popped the cork, then dumped half the bottle on the burning napkins. The flames sizzled and then went out.

Finally, Conor's eyes cleared and he gaped at the mess on the table. "What the hell were you doing?"

Olivia opened her mouth to explain, then snapped it shut. With a soft cry, she spun on her heel and ran into the bedroom, then slammed the door behind her. She sat down on the bed and clutched her trembling hands in her lap. What was she thinking? Did she really believe that she could seduce him with a candlelit meal and a bottle of champagne?

"Olivia?" A soft rap sounded on the door.

"Go away," she muttered, too embarrassed to even look at him. True, she'd never been good at seduction, but even a dope could turn a frozen tuna casserole into a nice meal without setting the apartment on fire.

"Come on," he said. "I didn't mean to snap at you. The smoke detector just startled me, that's all. Come on out and eat with me. The tuna casserole is getting cold."

Olivia drew her knees up under her chin. "I'm not hungry!"

The door opened and Conor peeked inside. He slowly approached the bed, then reached down and grabbed her hand. "If you ignore the smouldering napkins, the table looks very nice. And the food looks great." He gave her arm a tug and pulled her to her feet. "Come on."

He dragged her along to the living room, then settled her beside him on the floor. The smell of scorched paper mixed with the aroma of tuna casserole and spilled champagne. Conor picked up the candle and relit it with a soggy book of matches. "See, it looks good," he said as he scooped a spoonful of casserole onto her plate.

She ignored the food. "What are we doing here?"

Conor chuckled. "Well, a few minutes ago, you were torching our hideout. Now we're eating dinner."

"No," she murmured. "I mean, what are we doing? You're a cop and I'm a witness and all I can think about is plying you with tuna casserole and champagne so you'll kiss me again." She turned to him, meeting his eyes directly. "What's going to happen to us when this is all over?"

Conor's gaze dropped to the table and he picked up his fork and pushed the casserole around on his plate. "What do you mean?"

"You know what I mean. We have this attraction to each other. We slept together last night. Are we supposed to just stop when this is over and go on with our lives?"

Conor closed his eyes and released a tightly held

breath. "I don't know, Olivia. I didn't expect this to happen. It just happened."

"And as far as you're concerned, this is all wrong," Olivia said.

"It's not right," he muttered. "And I could probably lose my job because of it. But there's no going back, so I guess we shouldn't worry about it."

"There is a way to go back," Olivia said.

"And how is that?"

"We just have to stop this right now. Pretend it never happened." She stood up and smoothed her hands over her thighs, hating what she'd been forced to say, yet knowing in her heart it was the best thing for both of them. They couldn't go on without one of them getting hurt. "We can do that. Before it gets out of control."

"I think that ship has already sailed," he said.

"No, it hasn't," she replied firmly. "From now on, we go back to the way it was supposed to be. I'm the witness and you're the cop." She clutched her hands in front of her to stop the trembling, then forced a smile. "I—I think I should probably get some sleep—in my room, alone."

She'd slept away most of the afternoon and wasn't at all tired. But Olivia knew if she didn't walk away from Conor, didn't lock herself in her bedroom, then there would be no way to keep herself from wanting him. "I—I'll just be going," she said, taking a step back.

Olivia waited, hoping that he'd try to stop her, try to explain all the reasons why her plan would never work. But he just stared up at her, a look of resignation set on his handsome face. She felt as if her heart had been torn in two. How could she want him so much, yet know how serious the consequences were for him? And how could he want her so little that he could let her walk away?

"Good night," she murmured. Drawing a deep breath and gathering her resolve, she turned and walked to the bedroom. She closed the door behind her, waited for him to call her name, waited for an invitation back into his arms. But Conor remained silent and his silence told her all she needed to know.

He didn't want her. Or if he did, he was strong enough to resist. Olivia sat on the edge of the bed and drew a long, shaky breath. Now, if only she could find the same strength, then maybe she could get through this without losing her mind.

OLIVIA STOOD in the darkened living room for a long time, watching him sleep by the moonlight that filtered through the windows. It was nearly three o'clock in the morning and she hadn't slept a wink. But Conor wasn't having the same trouble. He was draped across the sofa, his arm thrown over his head and one foot resting on the floor. His naked chest rose and fell in an even rhythm and the quilt was twisted around his long legs.

She wanted to touch him one last time, to run her hands over his broad chest and trace a finger along the soft line of hair that ran from his collarbone to his belly. She wanted to take his face in her hands and kiss him, just to lose herself in the taste of his mouth for a moment or two.

But they'd made a decision and she had to stick to it. To give in to her impulses now would be pure weakness. Besides, the prospect of being turned away by Conor was too humiliating to even consider. She'd see that look in his eyes, that vague indifference, and he'd draw away, as if her touch meant nothing, or worse, as if he found it repulsive. No, she wouldn't subject herself to that.

Olivia turned to walk away, but she didn't see the coffee table in the dark. Her shin banged up against the heavy wood and she bit her lip to keep from crying out. Tears of pain pressed at the corners of her eyes and she muttered a silent string of curse words. The pain gradually subsided and she tested her leg. Though it hurt, she managed to take a few mincing steps.

"Olivia?"

She froze, holding her breath and hoping that Conor couldn't see her in the dark. He moved, the blankets rustling, and Olivia winced, knowing that she wouldn't get away without speaking to him. She slowly turned and forced a smile.

"What's wrong?" he murmured, brushing the sleep from his eyes. "Are you all right?"

"No," Olivia said.

He sat up. "What is it?"

"I—I was thirsty. I needed some water." It sounded like a good excuse, though the water was in the kitchen and not the living room.

His pushed to his feet, casting aside the quilt, and Olivia noticed that he wore only his boxers. She groaned inwardly. Why couldn't they have sent her a cop with a big belly and bowlegs, she wondered. Why had she been cursed with a man who had an impossibly muscular chest and a perfect narrow waist and legs that were almost nicer than hers?

"There's water in the kitchen," he murmured. "Would you like me to get you a glass?"

She drew a ragged breath and shook her head. "I don't want water," Olivia said, her voice trembling. "I—I want you." The words barely registered. What if he refused? What if she had to walk back to her bedroom all alone? "I—I can't sleep and I want you to come to bed with me."

Conor rubbed his forehead. "Olivia, I—"

"I know what you're trying to do," she said, taking a step toward him. "And I understand. But I know this would just be a stolen week. And that when we went back to the real world things would change. But we're not in the real world now." She took another step, putting herself just an arm's length away. "Make love to me, Conor, just once more, and I promise I won't ask again."

Conor moaned softly as he reached out his hand and skimmed his knuckles along her cheek. His touch sent her heart racing and, for a moment, she was certain he'd turn her away. But then he caught her in his embrace and drew her near. With trembling hands, she reached up and cupped his face in her palms. His beard was rough to her touch, but she smoothed her fingers over the planes and angles, determined to memorize every inch of the man she'd come to love.

He was capable of loving her, Olivia knew this. But with Conor it would take time. And time was in short supply for the two of them. All she could hope for was that once they were apart he'd realize the depth of his feelings for her and he'd come back. And tonight, she'd do what she could to make that happen.

Olivia stepped back, then reached for the hem of the T-shirt she wore and pulled it over her head. She stood before him, naked and unashamed. "Tell me what you want," she said.

"Why can't I stop this?" he whispered, closing his eyes and tipping his head back.

"Because you want me," she said. She grabbed his face and held him until he opened his eyes. "And I want you."

His eyes met hers and she saw the truth there. He didn't just want her, he needed her, as much as she needed him. Olivia reached up and brushed her hair from her shoulders. His gaze fell to her breasts, then raked along the length of her body. She felt wicked, wanton, her usual restraint gone.

She held out her hand. "Come to bed with me," she said.

He slipped his hands around her waist and pulled her against him. They kissed, clumsy at first, then more desperately. Her tongue grazed his bottom lip, probing, daring him to respond. And he did, his control shattering the moment their tongues touched.

But Olivia was in control and she pulled away, tracing a line of kisses across his jawline and down his neck. "Tell me you want me," she murmured, teasing at his nipple with her tongue.

He groaned softly. "I don't want you," he said. "I can't want you."

"But you do," she insisted. "And I can prove it."

Her fingers dropped to the waistband of his boxers

and she slowly pushed them down, the fabric catching on the evidence of his desire. He was hard and beautiful, and as she bent to slide his boxers down to his ankles, she kissed him there. The sharp intake of his breath broke the silence and Olivia stayed where she was.

Slowly, deliberately, she tasted his sex, running her tongue along the hard ridge and taking him into her mouth. It was so intimate, this pleasure she gave him, that she was certain he'd stop her. But Conor wove his fingers through her hair and held her, watching as she made love to him with her mouth, stilling her movement when it became too much for him to bear, gently urging her forward when he wanted more.

A moan rumbled in his chest and he grabbed her hands and pulled her to her feet. Frantic with need, he kissed her, his mouth taking possession of hers, demanding and intense. His erection pressed against her stomach, hot and wet from her mouth and she knew she'd brought him so close that just one more touch would take him over the edge.

"Tell me what you want," she whispered. "Tell me you want me."

He grabbed her waist and lifted her up, then wrapped her legs around his hips. "I want you," he said as he buried his face in the curve of her neck. The tip of his erection teased at her entrance. "So help me, I want you so bad I can't stand it."

Olivia tipped her head back and smiled, running her fingers through her hair. She hadn't been wrong. And when all was said and done, when their days together were over and they'd both gone back to their lives, he'd remember this passion between them. And he'd come looking for it again.

Conor carried her to the dining room table, where he'd tossed his shirt and jeans. He set her down on the edge of the table, then fumbled to find his wallet. Olivia grabbed the condom from his fingers and tore the foil package open. But he was impatient and he grabbed it from her and quickly sheathed himself, as if her touch was more than he could take.

Then Conor stepped between her legs and gently pushed her back onto the table, his mouth coming down on one of her nipples. Olivia sighed softly as he took control, delighting in the feel of his body pressed into her. Wave after wave of delicious sensation washed over her as he made love to her in the same way she had to him.

He found every spot that made her shiver with need and when he finally tasted her damp core, ran his tongue over her swollen nub, she was already near the edge of conscious thought. This was all she ever needed in her life, he was the only lover she'd ever wanted. And these feelings coursing through her body were as close as she'd ever come to paradise. "Please," Olivia murmured, reaching out for him, bringing his mouth back to hers. "Please."

He drew her closer to the edge of the table, his hands skimming over her breasts, then clasping her hips. Gently, with exquisite tenderness, he entered her. Olivia murmured his name and arched against him, needing him to fill her with his heat, wanting him to take her the rest of the way.

Conor drove deep, burying himself completely, then

slowly withdrew, as if to tease her, to make her shiver and ache for him. With each thrust, his rhythm increased, but he still wouldn't give in to his own desire. He was in control now, and though Olivia felt she was near her own climax, it was Conor who would determine when it came.

Suddenly, he stopped, his body tense, his expression restrained. Olivia moaned softly. "Don't," she murmured, wriggling against him, trying desperately to reach him with her hands.

With a low growl, he grabbed her wrists and pinned her arms above her head, still buried deep inside her. For a moment, Olivia thought it was over, that he'd brought her this far only to leave her wanting more.

But then he dropped a kiss on her lips, lingering a long moment before drawing away. "Tell me that you want me," he said, staring down into her eyes, his gaze intense.

"I want you," she murmured, tipping her head back and moaning as he slowly withdrew.

"Tell me again," he demanded, plunging into her.

"I do," Olivia breathed. "I need you, Conor. Please." She opened her eyes to find him staring at her. This time, his gaze was like a caress, his expression soft. He let go of her wrists and touched her cheek with his fingers. Then he drew a ragged breath. "Tell me that you love me," he said, his words hesitant. "Just for tonight, tell me."

Olivia felt the emotion surge inside of her at his simple request. And though he just wanted to hear the words, she knew there was much more there, in her heart and in her soul. And that there was a reason he needed to hear the words. "I love you," she murmured, holding his handsome face in her hands and staring into his eyes. "Just for tonight, I love you."

He smiled down at her, then kissed her ever so softly. "And I love you," he replied. "Just for tonight."

And when they finally both cried out their release, Olivia came to a startling realization. This man was part of her and she was part of him. They'd touched each other in a way that made them one. And no matter what happened to pull them apart, they would always have each other and this perfect time they had spent together.

THE NOISE woke him up. Conor was continually amazed how he could tell the difference between a threatening sound and background noise, even when he was sound asleep. His instincts immediately sharpened. Olivia was asleep beside him in her bed, her naked body curled against his, oblivious to the danger. He thought about waking her, then decided to investigate first.

Conor carefully crawled out of bed, then searched the floor for his gun. He found it on the bedside table, still tucked in his holster. He thought about getting dressed, just in case the intruder was one of Lila Wright's nosy friends. He compromised by pulling on a pair of boxer shorts.

He took slow steps to the bedroom door, then peered around the corner before starting down the hall. Sunshine illuminated the living room and dining room and the noises grew louder. If this was one of Keenan's men, he wasn't trying very hard to conceal his presence.

The sounds came from the kitchen, clanking utensils and running water. Conor pressed back against the wall as he made his way down the hallway. Then he drew a steadying breath and rushed the kitchen, his gun aimed chest high.

He smelled the freshly brewed coffee at about the same time that he shouted "Freeze!" at a pale-haired man in a leather jacket. The man's hands shot up and he ducked his head. It was only then that Conor recognized Danny Wright. He strung a few vivid curses together, then lowered his gun. "Damn it, I could have shot you!"

Danny slowly turned around, his hands still raised over his head. His gaze slowly took in Conor's disheveled appearance and his eyebrows shot up. But he didn't offer a comment. His only reaction was a slight blush of embarrassment.

"What the hell are you doing here?" Conor demanded.

"I had to talk to you," Danny said. "I knocked, but there was no answer. So I used my extra key. I figured after what you two have been up to, you were probably sleeping in." He paused. "I—I mean, all the excitement you've had. That is, the danger, not the excitement. I meant that—"

Conor raised his hand to stop the babbling that inevitably sprang from his partner's mouth right after he stuck his foot into it. He walked over to the counter and poured himself a mug of coffee, then turned around. "Why are you here?" he repeated.

"I—I just came to tell you that the D.A. cut a deal last night with Kevin Ford. He'll testify against Keenan in return for a plea bargain on his own charges. He was also interviewed by Internal Affairs and he gave them the name of the cop that tried to coerce him. Ford has papers and tapes and enough evidence to put Keenan away for a long time. Olivia won't have to testify."

"You're sure?" Conor asked.

"She was the only one to connect Ford to Keenan. With the evidence that Ford turned over, there'll be a lot of Keenan's associates who will be offering up testimony in exchange for deals. She should be safe."

"We're not sure of that," Conor said, suddenly faced with the fact that this might be their last day together. "Not until the trial."

"Word on the street is that Keenan has already cancelled the contract on her life."

Conor took a long sip of his coffee. This was it, then. He could take Olivia home this morning and they could both go on with their lives. What they shared together last night would fade into a distant memory. And he wouldn't have a chance to make her feel what he'd forced her to say last night—that she loved him.

Danny swallowed convulsively. "How's your side?"

Conor shrugged. He'd almost forgotten. Olivia had a way of making all his pain just disappear. "I'm all right."

"There is one other thing," Danny murmured. "The lieutenant wants to see you this morning."

"I suppose he wants to reprimand me for not checking in on a regular basis. Or maybe I'm going to have to pay for all those broken windows at the Happy Patriot?"

"I think it might be more serious than that." Danny paused. "Can I speak freely, sir?"

"Only if you stop calling me 'sir.' We're both detectives, Danny. We're partners. Although I may be a few years older than you, I don't outrank you."

Danny nodded, then continued. "You know the captain's not a big fan of yours. He's been looking for anything to bust you back down to a beat cop. He thinks you have no respect for authority. And after the incident with that con man, he's been gunning for you. There's talk that he's going to have you investigated, maybe brought up on charges."

"And why would he do that?"

"They found out about your visit to Kevin Ford and his lawyers claim that you might have threatened him."

"Did Ford tell them that?"

Danny shook his head, then gave Conor's appearance the once-over. "The captain also suspects that you and—" He cleared his throat. "You and the witness might have developed a...personal relationship. Is that true?"

"What do you think?" Conor muttered. Sure, it was true and it was very personal. It was more personal than he'd ever been with any other woman. And if that was a crime, then let him be guilty. "You don't have to answer that," he added.

"You're sleeping with her," Danny said. "And that's against just about every written and unwritten rule the Boston P.D. has. I want you to know that I like working with you and I'd be disappointed if something happened to put our partnership at risk."

Conor clapped Danny on the shoulder and smiled tightly. "You can talk to the lieutenant and tell him I'll be in later this morning. I'll answer whatever questions he has. And if the captain wants to investigate, he's welcome to do that. I've got nothing to hide."

"Danny!"

They both turned to find Olivia standing in the doorway to the galley kitchen. She was dressed only in Conor's flannel shirt, the tails barely reaching her thighs. Her hair was mussed and her lips slightly puffy. Conor wanted to pull her into his arms and kiss her, a perfect start to the day. But he held back. Last night was supposed to be the last time, he told himself.

"What are you doing here?" she asked. "Have you come to protect me?"

"Actually," Conor said, "Danny just stopped by to give me a message from my boss. He was just leaving, weren't you, Danny."

"But you can stay for coffee, can't you?" Olivia asked. "We haven't had much company." She walked into the kitchen and poured herself a mug of coffee. "I wanted to thank you for bringing over my things from the cottage on Cape Cod."

Danny grinned, instantly besotted with her. What was this power she had over men? Conor wondered. All she had to do was smile at them and they went soft in the head. "No problem. I took home that seafood stuff myself."

"The paella?"

Danny nodded. "It was really good. You're a good cook, Ms. Farrell."

She smiled. "Has the district attorney contacted you, Danny?"

"The district attorney?" Danny asked.

Conor shook his head, warning him off. "Danny really has to leave, Olivia. He's late for work."

She held the coffee in her hands and breathed in the steam. "But shouldn't I talk to the D.A. before I testify? I mean, that's what they do on television, isn't it? I can't just walk in there and answer his questions, can I? Doesn't he have to prepare me?"

Danny glanced back and forth between them, then smiled wanly. "Yes. I—I mean, I don't know. I guess that would depend."

Conor turned Danny around and pushed him out of the kitchen toward the door. "Aren't you going to tell her the good news?" Danny asked.

"Go back to the station," Conor murmured. "I'll see you later today." He pulled open the door, gently shoved Danny out, closing it behind him. Then he turned and leaned back against the door. Conor's mind turned over all the possibilities, all the ways he could tell her that their time together was over. But he couldn't. He needed more time, just another day or two, time enough to see if what they shared would last in the real world, time to see if there was any truth to the words he'd made her say the night before.

He wanted to believe Olivia could love him, but the real truth was staring him right in the eyes. They were from two different worlds. He was a cop, making a cop's salary and living a cop's life. She deserved more than that. She deserved a man who could stand beside her at her society parties, who could meet her rich friends and make intelligent conversation, not some guy who'd taken night courses to finish college and who preferred police reports to good literature.

"I probably shouldn't have come out when Danny was here," Olivia murmured.

Conor turned. Olivia stood in the dining room, looking delicate and vulnerable and completely kissable. But he held his ground. "No problem."

"What if he says something?"

"Danny knows when to keep his mouth shut," Conor said. He pushed off the door and walked into the dining room, then picked up his clothes. He was afraid to look at her again, afraid that he'd want to take her into his arms and make love to her for the rest of the day.

"I can make you some breakfast," Olivia said.

Conor smiled tightly. "That's all right. I wouldn't want you to set the kitchen on fire." He glanced up at her and saw disappointment suffuse her pretty face. He'd insulted her. "I'm sorry. I have to go. My boss wants to see me this morning and I can't keep him waiting."

Olivia nodded and she watched as he got dressed. By the time he pulled on his socks and shoes, her brow was furrowed and she was worrying at her lower lip with her teeth. Conor grabbed his jacket and his holster, then stepped over to her to drop a chaste kiss on her cheek. "Don't go out," he warned. "I'll be back in a little while."

When he reached the safety of the hallway, he leaned

back against the wall and took a deep breath. "You should just walk away now," he murmured to himself. "Just let her go while you still can."

It would be so easy. All he'd have to do was send an officer over to the condo to tell her the good news. She'd pack up and leave and he'd never have to see her again. But he couldn't bring himself to do that. He knew how much it would hurt Olivia.

No, he'd wait. Another day or two together was all he needed to find out for sure. And then they could leave this place and go on with their lives. And whether it was together or apart, Conor knew that he'd have given it a chance. That was all he could ask for—just a chance.

8

"WHY CAN'T WE go out?" Olivia asked. "The weather is beautiful. And no one has tried to shoot me for days. Why can't we go for a drive or just take a walk? We could go out for lunch! We'll drive way out in the country where no one could possibly recognize us. I'd even settle for drive-thru."

Conor looked up at her from behind his newspaper. He'd been strangely silent the past few days, distant, as if something weighed heavily on his mind. He'd made a few trips into the city and come back distracted, his face lined with tension, but when Olivia had asked what was wrong, he'd smiled and reassured her that everything was fine. She thought his worry might have to do with the trial and her testimony, that the danger to her wouldn't end at that. But she didn't want anything to interfere with the last few days they had together, so Olivia didn't press with her questions.

Their nights together hadn't changed. They'd both conveniently forgotten the promise they'd made and fallen into bed the very next night with as much passion as ever. Conor had been particularly uninhibited, making love to her each night until neither one of them could move, almost as if he were making love to her for the last time. After a night like that, she almost expected him to be gone in the morning. But Conor was always there when she woke, his limbs tangled with hers, his face nestled in the curve of her neck.

They hadn't mentioned the future, but Olivia knew with every day that passed they were coming closer to the time when they'd no longer have to be together. She'd expected that the district attorney would want to see her before she testified, but Conor hadn't mentioned anything about a meeting before the trial. She'd learned to trust him without question.

"Please," she begged, "put down your newspaper."

"All right," Conor said. He tossed aside the *Boston Globe* and levered up from the couch. "We'll take a drive. I'll show you my favorite spot in all of Boston."

Olivia clapped her hands, then raced to the bedroom to grab her jacket. She didn't care whether they were taking a risk. She needed to find out what life was like outside the condo. But, more importantly, she needed to find out what Conor was like when he wasn't standing guard or making love to her. They'd never really been out together and she needed a chance to gauge his feelings once they went back to the real world. Would he still touch her at every opportunity? Would he take her hand or drape an arm around her shoulders? Would he be at ease or would reality shatter the dream world they'd lived in for the past week?

She hurried out of the bedroom to find Conor waiting at the door. He opened it gallantly, then swept out his arm. "Your carriage awaits," he teased.

In truth, Olivia was surprised that he'd agreed to take her out at all. He was normally so vigilant, but maybe even he had started to go a little stir-crazy. When she stepped into the sunshine and the fresh air, she stopped and held her hands out. Then she closed her eyes and twirled around. "I feel like I've been released from prison," she cried. "It's a glorious day."

She ran to the car and Conor opened the door for her. Then he jogged around to the driver's side. Though the car wasn't Dylan's Mustang, it did move. And it was taking them out on an adventure! Olivia didn't care whether the muffler rumbled or the car shook when it went fast. She was with Conor and they were spending time in the real world. That was as close to heaven as she could imagine.

Conor drove through Concord, heading toward downtown Boston. Olivia stared out the window, watching the scenery pass by. Although she'd seen the same sights many times, everything looked so much brighter and prettier to her eyes. She hadn't realized how sheltered she had been, locked away from the hustle and bustle of everyday life.

"Where are we going?" she asked.

"You'll see," Conor replied with a smile.

She slid over the wide front seat to sit beside him, then slipped her arm through his and rested her head on his shoulder. "I know I'm going to have a good time, no matter where we go."

They rode most of the way in silence, enjoying the drive together. Conor steered the car off the freeway and soon they were winding along Boston's waterfront near the Fort Point Channel. Conor found a parking spot and they got out of the car and began to walk toward Waterfront Park. Olivia wove her fingers through his and they strolled hand in hand to a grassy spot near the water's edge.

"I used to come here when I was a kid," Conor explained. He sat down on the grass and pulled her down next to him, then smiled crookedly. "Come to think of it, I wasn't ever really a kid."

"You weren't?"

Conor shook his head. "Not after my ma left. When my da was out chasing swordfish around the North Atlantic, I'd have to find things to keep my brothers busy during the summer. Dylan and Brendan liked to get into trouble. So we'd take the 'T' and come out here and watch the planes all day. And if we had enough money, we'd ride the ferry back and forth to Logan. Sometimes we'd even go inside the airport, although security knew to look out for us."

"All by yourself?"

"I was sixteen and my brothers were used to listening to me. It was cheap entertainment. And it was a favorite trip. If I ever wanted my brothers to do something, all I had to do was promise them a trip out here to watch the planes. Brendan used to love this spot. He'd memorize plane schedules and he'd know where every plane was going. I think that's what gave him such wanderlust."

"You did a good job with them," Olivia said softly as she squeezed his hand. "They're all wonderful men. I don't even know them well, but I know that's true."

"Problem is, I didn't do such a good job on myself," he said, his smile turning ironic.

"That's not true," Olivia said.

Conor shrugged. "I never gave myself much chance to have fun. My brothers say I have to lighten up."

"We've had fun together," she said, "when we weren't getting shot at."

"But I never had fun when I was younger. Never went out on a date until I was nineteen. Girls didn't exactly enjoy five younger brothers tagging along everywhere I went. And I couldn't trust Dylan or Brendan to take care of the twins and Liam. So I was a stay-at-home brother. I guess that's why my social skills leave something to be desired."

"Well, I think you have other skills that make up for that," she said as she lay back on the grass.

Olivia stared up at the sky, a perfect shade of blue. She'd been to Waterfront Park before, but today was different. She was seeing it through Conor's eyes. As the planes roared overhead, heading out in different directions from Logan, Olivia could almost picture those six lost boys. He'd been a good parent to them, and he'd probably be an even better parent to his own children. She had never thought much about a family of her own. But sitting here next to Conor, she could imagine them with children.

"Olivia, there's something I need to tell you."

She opened her eyes to find him leaning over her, a serious expression on his face. Reaching out, Olivia placed a finger over his lips. "No," she murmured. "This day is perfect. I don't want to spoil it. There'll be time to talk later. I just want to enjoy the fresh air and the sunshine." She flopped back on the grass and stared up at the sky. "How could I have been so terrified just a week ago and so incredibly happy today? I just want it to last."

"I'm glad," he said, sitting back.

She shaded her eyes with her hand to study his face, then rolled over on her stomach. "What's it going to be like after I testify?" she asked. "Will I still have to worry about Keenan?"

"No," Conor said softly. "You won't have to worry about Keenan ever again."

"But what if he gets out and he decides he wants revenge?"

Conor took her hand and brought it to his lips, then placed a warm kiss on the inside of her wrist. "Then I'll protect you," he said.

His words were so simple and heartfelt that Olivia could almost believe he'd be there. "Will we see each other after the trial?" she asked.

Conor shrugged. "You'll be busy trying to get your business back on track. And you'll have your friends. You won't have any time to think about me."

"That's not true," Olivia said.

"It is," Conor replied. "Be honest, Olivia. If I'd walked up to you on the street and asked you out, you would have run in the opposite direction. You're from a different world, privileged, sophisticated, cultured. I'm just a cop and not a very good one at that."

"But that's not who I am," she said. "I didn't grow up on Beacon Hill. I grew up living above a little storefront in North End. My parents were hippies. They bought and sold what they called antiques, but what I'd probably call junk. We were poor, living hand-to-mouth. This me that you think you know is a me that I constructed from scratch. I read magazines to learn how to dress and studied books to understand my clients. I even took speech lessons so I could talk like I had money. I'm a complete fraud."

"But you belong in that world now," he said. "You've made a place for yourself with your high-society friends and your expensive antiques."

"But I like your world," she countered. "It's much more exciting. It makes me feel alive."

Conor shook his head. "I'll make you a deal. When this is over, we'll go back to our lives, and if you still feel the same way in a month, then we'll talk."

An entire month without Conor was unthinkable. She could barely pass an hour alone without craving the sound of his voice or the warmth of his touch. But Conor had wounds that went deep, wounds that made him distrust women. If he needed them to have time apart to prove her feelings, then that's what she'd give him. "Promise?" she asked. "Just a month?"

He nodded.

"I'll never regret what we shared," she said.

"Neither will I," Conor replied, dropping a quick kiss on her lips. "Neither will I."

THE LADIES had gathered around the table for morning coffee as was their habit but, today, they had invited themselves over to Olivia's apartment for the morning ritual. Olivia hadn't had the heart to refuse and, in all truth, she welcomed the company. She needed something—anything—to take her mind off Conor.

Since their field trip to the airport, things had changed, in some ways for the better, but in many ways for the worse. They'd become closer than ever emotionally, sharing stories from their pasts and spending the waking hours together in quiet conversation. They'd talked about his childhood, his parents, his early years in Ireland. She felt as if she'd been given a window into his soul and it was a rare gift. Conor wasn't one to let anyone see the real man beneath the indifferent exterior. She'd been allowed in.

But since that night when they had returned from Waterfront Park, Conor hadn't shared her bed. Like so many other topics of conversation, Olivia had been afraid to broach the subject with him. Besides, she suspected what he was doing. They only had a few more days together before the trial and he was preparing them both for the inevitable. Once the trial began, there'd be no more reason for them to be together. It was a sensible plan, Olivia thought, though it was hard to fall asleep without Conor exhausting her first with his lovemaking and then keeping her warm with his body. She'd been tempted to go to him, to ask him for one last night together. But she'd done that once and she couldn't bear to do it again.

Olivia drew a deep breath. She should have been satisfied with the new direction their relationship had taken—one where emotional intimacy had replaced physical pleasure. But over the past few days, she'd come to love Conor more than ever. And she wanted to express it in both words and actions.

Instead, Olivia found herself working out her frustrations by cooking. She made elaborate meals for them both. Conor, on the other hand, chose to exercise away his carnal feelings. Every morning, he headed out, only to return an hour later completely exhausted. And after a long shower, he'd run errands to the grocery store and the coin laundry and the gas station. Then, right before lunch, they'd leave for another field trip, an activity that had become a daily routine over the past three days.

Yesterday, they'd walked the Freedom Trail, something neither one of them had ever done, even though they'd both grown up in Boston. They wound their way through Boston, stopping at the Bunker Hill Monument and Paul Revere's house and the Old North Church. And the day before that, they'd visited the Museum of Science, then walked along the banks of the Charles until the sun had nearly set.

She'd managed to forget the upcoming trial, her worries fading into an occasional twinge of apprehension. Olivia wasn't sure how her life would change once she testified against Keenan and Kevin Ford, only that she couldn't imagine her future without Conor. She was madly in love with him and, for the first time in her life, she realized that there might be a man who could make her happy forever.

Olivia had tried to determine when her feelings had become so focused but, in truth, she couldn't remember a moment when she wasn't in love with Conor Quinn. They'd known each other just a week, yet she knew more about him than any other man she'd ever loved—or thought she'd loved.

She knew now that those other men had all been passing moments in her life, marking time until she was destined to meet Conor. Suddenly, her decision to testify made sense, as did all the other crazy things that had happened since she'd first called the police. This had all been part of a cosmic plan so that she could find the man she was supposed to love.

"My goodness, dear, you look like you're a million miles away," Sadie said.

Olivia blinked, then glanced around the table at the five elderly ladies who'd gathered for coffee and Danish. They were all staring at her. "I—I'm sorry. What were you saying?"

"Where is that gorgeous husband of yours?" Doris asked.

"He went out for a run. He likes to get some exercise in the morning. And sometimes in the evening, too. Can I get anyone else coffee?"

They all shook their heads and she noticed that all their cups were full and their Danish untouched. The five of them—Sadie, Doris, Ruth Ann, Geraldine and Louise—stared at her expectantly. "Go ahead," Ruth Ann whispered, giving Sadie an elbow. "Ask her."

"Ask me?" Olivia murmured, picking up her glass of orange juice. "Ask me what?"

Sadie smiled brightly. "So tell us, dear, how is the sex?"

Olivia's eyes went wide at the same moment her orange juice went down the wrong pipe. She coughed, covering her mouth and looking at the ladies through watery eyes. "Sex?"

Geraldine leaned forward, staring at Olivia through her bifocals. "Yes, dear. Tell us, is there anything new out there? All of us have been out of the loop, so to speak. And we like to keep up on new...trends."

"And it's obvious you're doing something right," Ruth Ann said. "That man of yours always looks so satisfied." She reached over and patted Olivia's hand. "Don't be embarrassed, dear. Sex is a regular topic of conversation with us."

Olivia forced a smile, a warm blush rising on her cheeks. "Ladies, I really don't think—"

"Maybe if I picked up a few new tricks," Louise said, "my George wouldn't always be making eyes at that hussy, Eleanor Harrington. Ever since her husband died, she's been on the prowl."

The other ladies nodded their heads in sympathy. "With the ratio of women to men at Waterbrook, it's a dog-eat-dog world," Sadie said. "I have to keep my Harold under lock and key for fear that one of those widows might charm him away."

"So how is it you keep your man happy?" Doris asked. "Do you cook him special foods? I hear oysters are supposed to make a man very randy."

Olivia swallowed hard. "Randy?"

"Oh, Doris, I've tried oysters and Harold just got gas," Sadie said. "I think there must be some new techniques. I see the books at the bookstore, although I'd never be caught dead taking one to the checkout counter. *How to Drive Your Man Wild in Bed.* It's one thing to discuss it over coffee, but can you believe someone would write about that?"

"I wonder if they'd have that one at the library," Louise asked.

The door to the condo opened and Conor strode in, dressed in sweatpants and running shoes, his damp T-shirt tossed over his shoulder. He'd left before the ladies had arrived and Olivia hadn't bothered to tell him about her plans for entertaining, certain he'd disapprove. "Hi, darling!" she cried, jumping up from her spot at the table.

Conor glanced between her and the ladies, who were staring at him with undisguised appreciation. He gave them all a quick glance, then planted a clumsy kiss on Olivia's lips, surprising them both.

The ladies giggled amongst themselves and Conor smiled at them all. "Good morning, ladies. How are you today?" They giggled again, like a bunch of shy schoolgirls. He gave them an odd look, then turned to Olivia. "Could I speak to you in the bedroom?"

Olivia followed him down the hall, then closed the door behind her. All of his things were scattered around her bedroom, tossed inside before the ladies had arrived. "I'm sorry, I know you don't want me talking to the neighbors, but—"

"No," Conor said, staring at the piles of clothes. He spied his jeans, then picked them up and rummaged through the pockets. "Where are my keys?"

"No?"

He picked through a pile of clothes until he found yesterday's flannel shirt. Then he checked that pocket. "No," he repeated. "I don't mind. Do you know where my keys are?"

Olivia stepped over to the dresser and grabbed the keys, then held them out to him. "They were in your shoe underneath the coffee table. I—I had to clean up before the ladies arrived."

Conor glanced up distractedly. "I have to go," he said. "Are you going to be all right here alone?"

"I thought we were going to go out to—"

"No, we can't. I've got business to take care of down

at the station house. I'm going to run home first and shower and change. I'll probably be gone most of the day."

"Is this about the trial?" Olivia asked.

"No. It's just some business that I have to take care of." He pulled the door open, then started off down the hall, Olivia right on his heels.

"Conor, wait."

He stopped and turned to her at the front door, then glanced over her shoulder at the ladies. With a tight smile, he bent close and placed another awkward kiss on her lips. "I'll see you in a little while, darling." He gave the ladies a wave and then walked out, leaving Olivia to wonder just what was so important that it preoccupied his thoughts so completely.

"Bye," she murmured, closing the door behind him. Olivia slowly walked back to the table and took her place.

Sadie sighed. "I suppose the honeymoon has to be over sometime, dear."

Olivia forced a smile, then reached for the pitcher of orange juice. As she poured herself a glass, she noticed the little bouquet of flowers that Geraldine had brought over to brighten the table. The daisies were placed in a faux silver tankard that had a remarkably realistic patina. Olivia reached for it and plucked a daisy out, then began to pull the petals off one by one. He loves me, he loves me not, she chanted silently.

The ladies continued to chat while Olivia listened with half an ear. She picked up the tankard and idly studied the design. For a reproduction, it really was quite remarkable. The weight was almost perfect for one of real silver. Usually she could tell real Colonial silver from reproduction without a second glance, but this piece almost left her guessing.

"Where did you get this?" Olivia asked. She held it up and stared at the bottom, looking at the mark. Her stomach did a quick flip-flop and she tried to remain calm.

"At the supermarket," Geraldine said. "I love fresh flowers and they have bouquets of daisies and carnations and mums for $3.99. They last nearly a week."

"Not the flowers," Olivia said. "The silver tankard."

Geraldine stared at it for a moment. "Oh, I don't know. I used to go to a lot of rummage sales when Louis and I were first married. We didn't have much money so I had to decorate on a budget. I must have picked it up then."

"At a rummage sale?"

"What difference does it make? It's just a cheap little thing, but I always thought it made a pretty vase."

Olivia pushed up from the table. "Would you mind if I borrowed this for a while?"

Geraldine's brow wrinkled in confusion but she nodded. "Why, certainly. In fact, if you'd like it, you can have it."

Olivia shook her head. "I—I don't think you want to give this to me," she murmured. Excitement pulsed through her, the same thrill she got whenever she found a hidden treasure. She'd wondered if she'd ever get that feeling back again, and here it was, as if it were simply part of her nature. "I have to go into Boston, but Conor has the car."

"Is there something wrong?" Sadie asked.

"No," Olivia said. "In fact, there might be something really right. I just need to check it out first. Can one of you take me to the train station?"

"What is it, dear?" Sadie asked.

"It's this," Olivia said, holding up the tankard. "Geraldine, I think this might be very valuable. I'm not sure yet, so I have to check some books."

"Valuable?" Geraldine said. "That old thing? How valuable?"

"Very," Olivia said. She turned from the table and grabbed her purse and jacket from the couch in the living room. "So who can take me?"

Sadie smiled, then clapped her hands. "Why, we'll all take you. This is very exciting. A valuable treasure right in our midst. Come on, ladies, let's go. We'll get the details in the car." With that, all five of them hurried out the door. Olivia glanced around the apartment, then wondered whether she should leave a note for Conor.

In the end, she decided not to. It would take her an hour at the most to get downtown on the train and an hour to get back. She'd only need a few minutes at the shop and she'd have her answers. No, she didn't need to leave a note. She'd be back in plenty of time.

FOR ONCE in his career, Conor wished he was back in a patrol car. At least he'd have a siren and lights to clear the way. But instead, he was stuck with the heap that his brother had procured, a car that shimmied over the speed of fifty and cornered as if the street were covered with Crisco.

He'd arrived home from his meeting with the brass

to find the apartment empty. At first, he'd assumed that Olivia had gone over to one of the ladies' apartments for whatever it was they did together. But when he knocked on Sadie's door, she informed him that they had taken Olivia to the train station and that Olivia was on her way into Boston.

The first thought Conor had was that she'd somehow found out about Kevin Ford, that she wouldn't have to testify and that their past four days together had been stolen time. He knew in his heart he shouldn't have lied to her and the guilt had been killing him. He'd wanted to tell her the truth, been tempted to tell her nearly every hour of every day.

But after that wonderful night on the dining room table, he knew that he couldn't let her go. She might be able to forgive him for wanting more time, but she might never forgive him for taking advantage of that time. Conor cursed softly.

He'd always had such a strong moral compass. What had happened to it? Since he'd met Olivia, he'd done things that would have once been unthinkable, bucking department regulations, falling in love with a witness, then deceiving a woman he'd come to love. But he'd done everything for the right reasons, in the hopes that Olivia might want a future with him.

Charles Street, as always, was bustling with shoppers and workday pedestrians and even a few groups of tourists. Conor double-parked, not even caring that the cops might tow the heap he was driving. He found the front door to Olivia's shop locked. Peering through the windows, he couldn't see anything in the dark interior except the shadowy forms of huge pieces of furniture—no movement, no light, nothing.

His heart slammed in his chest, his instincts on alert, but then he remembered there was no longer any danger. He wouldn't find Olivia inside, lying in a pool of blood. Keenan had called off his dogs and she had nothing to fear. He pounded on the door and waited impatiently. Sadie had mentioned something about a silver tankard and a special mark. He'd assumed she'd come to the shop, but maybe she'd gone home—or to one of the museums or libraries.

Conor hammered on the door again with his fist and, a few moments later, he heard a voice coming from inside. "We're closed," Olivia called.

"Olivia, let me in. It's Conor."

An instant later, the door swung open and Olivia stood in the doorway. "Conor!"

Conor stepped by her and walked into the shop. He glanced around, curious as to what it was she did for a living and impressed by the assortment of antiques in her shop. Even in the dim light he could see the fine quality of the furniture, the careful craftsmanship. This was her world, a world completely unknown to him. Hell, he had a twenty-year-old sofa and a coffee table he'd found in the alley behind his house. He reached over and grabbed the price tag for a huge wardrobe. It cost more than he made in a year.

"I'm sorry I left," Olivia said softly. "I—I thought I'd be back before you returned."

Conor turned and found her staring up at him, a frightened look on her face. Good grief, she still thought Keenan was after her. And she still believed that what she'd done would bring out his temper. He never, ever wanted to see that look of fear in her eyes again.

"Please don't be angry. I was careful," she said.

"I'm not angry with you," Conor replied.

"I just had to come. I wasn't sure about the mark but I knew I had a book here to check it out." She held up the tankard. "I thought I'd never feel this way again, Conor. Every time I remembered what I did for a living, I just got sad and depressed that it was all over. And then I saw this and I got that old feeling."

"Feeling?" he asked.

"It's like a little flutter in my stomach, a little lurch of excitement. Usually, I try to contain it, to tell myself that I might be too optimistic. But it's like digging in your garden and discovering gold."

"And this is all over a beer mug?"

Olivia sighed dramatically and rolled her eyes. "It's a silver tankard. And it's a Revere," she said, her voice full of awe and wonderment.

"A Revere? Like Paul Revere?"

"Not *like* Paul Revere," she repeated. "It *is* Paul Revere. He was a silversmith. His pieces have turned up in the oddest places, buried in peoples' backyards, hidden in walls. Do you have any idea how much this is worth? There are so few of these that have survived. When an original piece comes on the market, people take notice."

Conor stared down at her, the excitement suffusing her face making his guilt more acute. She looked so happy, so alive. She was doing something she loved, excited about the possibilities. He glanced around the shop at all the fancy furniture with the expensive price tags. This was her world. This was where she belonged and he'd kept her from this, from everything she'd loved. "Olivia, we need to talk."

"Geraldine was putting flowers in a Paul Revere silver tankard. Do you know what this means? I can put it up for auction and everyone will come to see it here in my shop before it's sold. The prestige of having this in my shop will do wonders to restore my reputation." She reached up and placed her palm on his cheek. "Please, don't be mad at me. I know I took a risk but—"

"No," Conor interrupted.

"No?" Olivia asked.

"There's no risk," he murmured. "That's what I came here to tell you."

She frowned. "What do you mean?"

"You're free," he said, the words burning in his throat. "Kevin Ford agreed to testify. Ford's got all sorts of incriminating evidence against Keenan and his whole wiseguy family. They're all scrambling over each other to see who can be the first to cut a deal. So you're off the hook."

Olivia let out a long breath, then smiled in amazement. "I don't have to testify?"

"You don't have to testify," Conor murmured.

With a squeal of delight, she threw herself at Conor and hugged him fiercely. Then she kissed him long and hard until he had no choice but to respond. When she finally pulled back, she was breathless with excitement. "I can't believe this. It's all over. I can get back to a real life."

A real life, Conor mused. Her words were like a dagger to his heart. A life without him. A life living among her expensive antiques and society friends. "So, I guess this is it," he said, schooling his voice into indifference. "I can have your things from the condo delivered to your house. And I'll make sure Tommy gets back home, safe and sound. And once—"

"You're talking like we're never going to see each other again," Olivia interrupted, her eyes wide, her mouth still damp from the kiss they shared.

Conor gently set her away from him and stared down into her wide eyes. "Remember that deal we made? The one where we go our separate ways, and then if you still feel something for me in a month, we can talk? Well, I was thinking we should do that. Only not for a month, but maybe for three or four?"

Conor saw the hurt in her eyes, and he knew he'd caused it, yet he couldn't take back the words. He hardened his heart and shored up his resolve. Once she went back to her world, she'd forget all about him.

"I don't like that deal," Olivia said stubbornly.

Conor sighed. She wasn't going to make this easy. "I've been suspended, Olivia. That's what I found out today at a meeting with my boss. There's going to be an investigation into my...improper behavior."

"You saved my life!" Olivia cried. "How can that be improper?"

"You were a witness and I exerted undue influence. I developed feelings for you when I knew it was wrong. I ignored departmental procedure. I figure my career with the Boston Police Department is probably over."

"That doesn't matter," Olivia said, reaching out to touch his arm. "I don't care if you're a cop or not."

"But I do," Conor said, evading her touch. "Just like this is who you are, a cop is who I am. If I'm not a cop, then I've got nothing."

"You have me," Olivia insisted.

"But I don't have anything to offer you. Come on, Olivia, at least you should know that much about me. I have to take care of the people I love. I can't let them take care of me."

She blinked once, her gaze fixed on his. "Then you admit it?"

"Admit what?"

"You love me," she said. "And I love you. And we can get through this."

Conor shook his head, then cupped her cheek in his hand. He wanted to believe in the truth in her words, but all this had happened so quickly between them. People didn't fall in love in a week. And those who did usually fell out of love just as quickly. "I have to get through this on my own. And I think you need time to realize that what we had didn't ever exist in the real world. You live in the real world, Olivia, where people like you don't socialize with cops."

"Please, don't leave me," she said, her eyes filling with tears.

"Give it time," he murmured, taking a step back. The very effort made his heart twist in his chest. Then he turned and walked toward the door. A muffled sob echoed through the shop and he cursed himself for hurting her. But it was better this way. She would hurt for a few days and then she'd realize that she never really loved him at all.

When he reached the street, he stopped, fighting the urge to go back in and kiss away all his doubts. "Give it time," Conor murmured as he started toward the car. "Just give it some time."

9

CONOR STOOD outside Quinn's Pub, staring at the building from across the street. Neon beer signs blazed from the plate-glass windows and Irish music drifted out every time the door opened. His brothers had insisted that he meet them for a drink and he already knew what was going on inside. The pub had played host to many celebrations. Any excuse to hoist a pint or two was welcomed at Quinn's. But this time, the celebration was meant for Conor.

Earlier that morning, Detective Conor Quinn's suspension had been lifted. The investigation into the improprieties in the Red Keenan case had been dropped and he was told to be back on the job the next morning. As far as his superiors cared, he'd been guilty of nothing more than poor judgment. Conor sighed softly, his breath clouding in the cold, damp fog that had fallen over Boston. So that was the end of it. Poor judgment.

Somehow, it seemed to be an awfully simple explanation for such a complex time in his life. Hell, a little more than three weeks ago, he'd arrived at that cottage on Cape Cod to do a job. And in the process of doing his job, he'd fallen in love with the most incredible woman he'd ever known. He'd spirited her away, safe-guarding her life while violating a host of departmental policies and procedures. And even after the danger was over, he'd tricked her into believing that she still needed his protection.

Poor judgment didn't even begin to describe his actions over the past few weeks. He'd been crazy, out of his mind, wrapped up in a world that was pure fantasy. Yet here he was, standing in front of Quinn's, back to his old life and his old ways, ready to spend his evening lost in a bottomless glass of Guinness while he recounted his regrets.

He'd thought about calling Olivia. The trial had begun and was over within three days, Red Keenan choosing to plea bargain against overwhelming evidence provided by his associates. Kevin Ford had never even had to testify, yet he walked as a result of his own plea bargain. In the end, protecting Olivia had become a moot point and everything that they'd shared now existed in a strange limbo between real life and fantasy.

Chances were, Olivia had already settled back into her life. He'd once thought he could be a part of that future, but then he'd been hit with the Internal Affairs investigation. With his job in jeopardy, Conor had believed that he'd had nothing to offer her. But now that he had his job back, he'd begun to fantasize that maybe they could make it work.

She'd never really disappeared from his life. Every hour of every day, he thought about her, replaying their time together over and over again in his head, until he could recite their conversations by heart. He'd learned to conjure up an image of her face, a memory of her scent and her taste, the sound of her laughter, by just closing his eyes and allowing his mind to drift.

At night, when he lay in bed alone, his hands could

still feel her silken skin and the soft contours of her naked body molded against his. The memories were so intense that he wondered if they'd ever fade. In truth, he didn't want them to. He wanted to make more memories, a lifetime full of memories with Olivia.

Yes, things had changed. But he still couldn't bring himself to contact her. Hell, she was probably better off without him. Now that she was back to her old life, she probably barely thought of him. And he'd never been the sort to settle down into domestic bliss.

Conor cursed softly. But he could be. With Olivia in his life, he could be a loving husband and a terrific father. He wasn't sure how he knew for certain, but Conor was sure he **ha**d what it took to make her happy. She'd given him that, a glimpse inside his heart, a realization that he could love—and be loved—without fear. Olivia wasn't Fiona Quinn, and if they had a life together, he'd never do anything to make her run away.

He had control, Conor mused. If he wanted to make a relationship work with Olivia, then he could make it work. Conor glanced up and down the street. Suddenly, he needed to see her, to hear her voice and to touch her face. He could make it happen if he just told her how he felt. Conor started toward his car, determined to find her and convince her that he loved her.

"Damn it!"

The sound of a voice on the empty street stopped him short. Only then did he notice a woman bent down on the pavement a few cars away. She seemed to be struggling with a tire iron. A few minutes earlier, he might have been glad for a diversion and an excuse not to go inside the pub. Now that he'd decided to find

Olivia, he was anxious to leave. But his duties as a cop couldn't be put aside. If there was a citizen in distress, he was bound to render aid. He hurried over to the spot. Changing a tire. How long could that take? "Can I help?"

The woman screamed, then jumped to her feet, clutching the tire iron in her fist.

Conor held out his hands. "It's all right," he said. "I'm a cop. I can help you."

The young woman regarded him warily, raising the tire iron a few more inches. "Let me see your badge," she demanded, the tremor in her voice giving away her fear.

Conor impatiently reached into his pocket and withdrew the leather case, then flipped it open. He should have just walked away. She obviously didn't want his help. "See," he said. "Detective Conor Quinn. Boston P.D."

She blinked in surprise. "Quinn?" Her gaze darted across the street.

"Yeah," Conor said. "My da owns Quinn's Pub." He stared at her for a long moment as the light from the streetlamp caught her face. A strange sense of déjà vu flashed though his mind, so brief that he wasn't able to focus on it. "You look familiar. Have we met?"

She shook her head. "No. Never."

But Conor had an eye for faces, a skill well honed by his career as a cop. And he knew he'd seen this woman before. Not in the smoky interior of the bar and not at the bustling squad room at the station, but on a street, in the dark, much like this. "Are you from the neighborhood?" he asked.

"Yes," she said, answering a bit too quickly for his liking.

If she lived in the neighborhood then she should have known it wasn't the best idea for her to be changing a tire—alone—on a dark street in Southie, she hadn't hesitated to threaten him with a tire iron. "Where?" he asked.

She pointed off to the west. "Over in that area. Do you think you could help me change my tire? I—I'm in a big hurry."

Conor took the tire iron from her hand and turned his attention to the stubborn lug nuts. This was exactly what he wanted to be doing right now, getting his hands dirty doing his duty as an officer of the law for a citizen who was obviously lying to him. Once he had the nuts all loosened, he quickly jacked the car up and finished removing them. But his mind really wasn't on the task at hand. Instead, he was determined to remember where he knew this woman from.

He grabbed the tire and wrestled it off the bolts, then rolled it to the rear of the car. She wasn't really a woman, but then she wasn't a girl either. She seemed to be caught in between. Her dark—almost black—hair was cropped short and her delicate features made her look much younger than she probably was. But it was the eyes that made Conor curious. Though she knew he was a cop, they still held a large measure of apprehension and indecision.

"You know, you could have just come into the bar," he suggested, "and used the phone to call a friend. You shouldn't be out on a dark street like this alone." He grabbed the spare and rolled it toward the front of the car.

"I don't have any friends," she murmured. "I—I mean, not in the neighborhood. Not home. They're all...out. So is the bar a family business?"

Conor glanced over his shoulder. "Me and my brothers all take turns working on the weekends."

"Brothers?" she asked. "You have brothers? How many?"

Conor frowned. For a stranger who lived in the neighborhood but didn't know exactly where she lived, and didn't have any friends, she certainly was curious. As he replaced the lug nuts, a slow realization dawned. So that was it! She was probably one of Dylan's girls or maybe a friend of Brendan's. His brothers always had women hanging around, giggling and whispering over them, staring at them with cow eyes. The poor girl probably had a crush and was waiting outside, hoping to catch a glimpse of whichever Quinn she'd fallen in love with.

"I have five brothers," he said, wondering which one she was interested in hearing about. Most girls gravitated toward Dylan, swept away by the notion of being with a real live hero. But there were others who found Brendan's lust for danger too attractive to resist. And then there were Sean, Brian and Liam, each of them holding their own particular charms.

"Five brothers," she said. "I—I can't imagine having five brothers. What are their names?"

Conor stood and brushed off the knees of his jeans, then moved to release the jack. "Dylan, Brendan, Sean, Brian and Liam." Her eyes went wide and Conor couldn't help but feel sorry for the poor girl. She had it bad for a Quinn. It really didn't matter much which one, since his little brothers weren't in the market for love and Conor had already been taken. "They're all inside waiting for me. Why don't you come in? You can wash your hands and I'll buy you a soda."

She shook her head as if the notion of going inside with him was completely improper. "No!" she cried. "I have to go. I'm late." She grabbed the tire iron from his hand then scrambled to drag the jack from beneath the bumper. She tossed them both in the back seat then ran to slam the trunk shut. A few seconds later, she roared off down the street, without the flat tire and without even giving Conor a "thank you" for his efforts.

"You're welcome!" he shouted after her car. He stood on the sidewalk, racking his brain, trying to figure out how he knew her. She looked so familiar. And then he remembered. It had been that night he'd stopped at the pub before heading out to Cape Cod. She'd been walking on the sidewalk in front of the pub and he'd nearly knocked her over. The odd thing was, he'd thought he recognized her that time, too.

Conor shook the memory from his brain, then glanced across the street at Quinn's. The only woman he wanted to think about right now was Olivia Farrell. And his only concern right now was finding her and telling her how much he cared. Everything else could wait for later.

"KEVIN!"

Olivia stood in the middle of the showroom of the Charles Street store and stared at her former partner. He was the last person she had expected to see! He looked a bit thinner and his complexion had lost its ruddy tone, but he was still the same man. Only now, he was an admitted criminal.

"Hello, Olivia," he murmured, a faint blush rising to his pale cheeks.

She crossed her arms over her chest, not sure if she ought to be afraid or angry. "What are you doing here?"

He shrugged, then glanced around the shop. "I'm out," he said. "I cut a deal to testify against Keenan and against the cops that he'd bought off. But then Keenan cut a deal and I never had to take the stand. I'm a free man."

"I suppose I should thank you," Olivia said. "If it weren't for you, I'd have had to testify."

His gaze dropped to his expensive Italian loafers. "I'm sorry about that, Olivia. I should have stood up and taken responsibility for what I'd done rather than pass off my problem to you. It was my fault, but now I'll pay the price. I'll be the one looking over my shoulder for the rest of my life, wondering if one of Keenan's associates might be following me."

"I suppose you expect to pick up where we left off," she said, a defensive edge to her voice. Olivia straightened her spine. "Well, I don't want to do that. I've gone through our inventory and separated our acquisitions. I'm going to take my stock and start over somewhere else. I'll be out by the end of the month."

"That's what I wanted to talk to you about," Kevin said. "My credibility is pretty much shot in this town. I want to turn over my client list to you and I want to give you the shop. You can take over the mortgage." He shook his head, a sardonic smile curling his mouth. "You were always better at this business, anyway. You can take my name off the sign. I'd just ask one thing."

"What's that?" she asked, her mind racing at this new development.

"That you let me sell through your shop. I'm going to be moving around a lot and I need a way to make a living. I'll send you stock from around the country and you sell it, on consignment. You'll get a cut of everything you sell."

Olivia thought about the proposal for a long moment. It was a perfect plan. She could keep the Charles Street shop, a location that she'd never be able to replace. And she wouldn't have to pack up all her stock and pay for the move. And Kevin really wasn't asking for much, just a way to make a living. Didn't she owe him at least that much?

"Why would you do this for me?"

"Because it's the right thing to do," he said. "I'm going to have my lawyer call you and make all the arrangements. And you can expect stock whenever I find something interesting." He stepped toward her as if to kiss her on the cheek, but settled for a pat on her arm. Then Kevin turned and walked toward the door.

"What made you change your mind about testifying?" she called, just as he reached for the knob.

"A visit from a cop named Quinn."

Olivia blinked in surprise. "Conor Quinn? He convinced you to testify?"

Kevin shrugged. "He came to see me about ten days or so before the trial was scheduled to start. He was concerned for your safety. I decided to cut a deal right after I talked to him."

She frowned, her mind troubled by the admission. It didn't fit. "Are you saying that Conor knew I didn't have to testify a week and a half before the trial started?"

Kevin nodded. "He and his partner worked with me to put together the deal. It only took a day for my lawyer to convince the D.A. that I had something to trade for a suspended sentence." He stared at her for a long moment. "He's in love with you, you know."

"What?" Olivia asked, her gasp echoing in the silent shop.

"That's why he was so determined to keep you from testifying. He loves you. Believe me, I know the signs." He paused, a look of regret washing over his face. "And if I don't miss my guess, you're in love with him."

The moment he said the words, Olivia realized the truth in them. She'd known in her heart how *she* felt, but gauging the depth of Conor's emotions was almost impossible. But perhaps she shouldn't have waited to hear the words. Instead, she should have known from his actions. He'd kept her close, even after the threat to her life had been eliminated. She could only hope that he'd done that because he couldn't bear to let her go.

"I—I have to talk to him," Olivia said. "I have to see him." She tossed aside the clipboard she'd been using for inventory, then grabbed her coat from a nearby Empire settee. "You have a key. Lock up before you leave."

She had no idea where Conor lived, his phone number was unlisted, and she didn't have the time to call every precinct house in Boston, if he hadn't been thrown off the force. She only knew one place to go— Quinn's, his family's pub. She got the address from the phone book, then hurried out the front door. Her breath came in quick gasps as she ran down the sidewalk and she could feel herself trembling with anticipation.

She was taking a chance going to him. They'd only been apart ten days. But Olivia had to believe he cared, that, if confronted, he'd be forced to admit his true feelings. Perhaps she should play harder to get, wait for him to come to her. But she knew Conor well enough to know that probably wouldn't happen. And now that she'd decided she wanted to spend the rest of her life with him, she wanted their life together to start right away.

Her car was parked at home, so she grabbed the first cab that she saw and directed him to South Boston. They skirted around the edge of the Public Gardens and wound their way to the Broadway Bridge, her mind going over everything she planned to say. She still wasn't sure how to begin. She could just blurt out that she was madly in love with him, then leave it to Conor to respond. Or she could list all the reasons why they belonged together. Or perhaps a better strategy would be to throw herself into his arms and kiss him and show him why he couldn't live without her.

Once she crossed into Southie, Olivia peered out the windshield of the cab, squinting to read the street numbers above the taverns that she passed. Though she'd never been to Southie in all the years she'd lived in Boston, she didn't think finding Quinn's Pub would be difficult. It was located just off Broadway, the main thoroughfare. But then a person couldn't spit in Southie without hitting an Irish pub.

The street was lined with cars, and as she stepped out of the cab and paid the cabbie, she could hear music drifting through the misty night air. The sound of an Irish band, a fiddle, a flute and a drum, drew her closer. Before she reached for the door, she smoothed her hands through her hair, then she drew a deep breath. No matter what happened, this moment would change her life forever.

She stepped inside and found herself in the middle of a party. The Irish band was playing on a small stage at the far end of the long, narrow bar and people stood shoulder to shoulder, talking and laughing. She glanced around, praying she'd find a familiar face, hoping that Conor would appear out of the crowd and sweep her off her feet.

"Olivia?"

She spun around to see Brendan standing at the end of the bar, waving in her direction. Relief washed over her. It was only then that she noticed Dylan sitting next to him and Sean and Brian, the twins, behind the bar. A moment later, Liam appeared out of the crowd.

She pushed through the crush of people to the spot where the Quinn brothers had congregated. Brendan gave her a quick kiss on the cheek and Dylan slipped off his stool to give her a place to sit.

"I'm looking for Conor," she said nervously. "Is he here?"

Brendan laughed. "Nope. We're all waiting for him. This party is in his honor."

"A party for Conor? For what?"

"A work thing. He's back on the job," Dylan explained. He paused, then winced as if he realized he'd probably spoken out of turn. "He didn't tell you about the Internal Affair investigation?"

Olivia nodded. "He did. But Conor and I haven't

seen each other for a while. Since the case is done, there's no reason to..." She drew a shaky breath. "I just need to talk to him." She stood up. "Can you tell me where he lives?"

"You stay here," Dylan said. He pushed away from the bar. "We'll find him for you. Brendan, you check his apartment. I'll stop by the precinct and see if he's still working. Sean and Brian, why don't you check out his favorite cop bars? And Liam, you keep Olivia company. Get her something to eat and drink. This damn party was for him and it's about time he showed up, whether he wants to or not."

Olivia watched as they all strode to the front door, tall and dark and each one as handsome as Conor. She turned back to Liam and forced a smile, then folded her hands in front of her on the scarred wooden bar. "I guess I'll have a soda while I wait."

Liam sent her a devilish smile. "You're sittin' in Quinn's Pub, lassie. You'll have a Guinness or you'll have nothing at all."

CONOR STEPPED OUT of his car in front of Quinn's Pub for the second time that night. The street was dark and quiet, almost eerily so in the heavy fog. The bar had closed fifteen minutes ago, but Conor knew a few of his brothers would still be inside, ready to draw him a Guinness.

He'd been all over the city in search of Olivia. He'd even had his buddy at dispatch put out an APB on her car only to find it parked down the block from her house on St. Botolph Street. He'd stopped at her flat twice, checked the shop three times and had even knocked on Mrs. Callahan's door, wondering if she might know anything about Olivia's whereabouts. The landlady had regarded him suspiciously, as if he were there to return Tommy to her care. Once she was certain he didn't have the cat with him, she grudgingly told him that she hadn't heard from Olivia since she'd paid her rent a week ago.

He slowly strolled across the wet street toward the pub. Now that Red Keenan was incarcerated and awaiting sentencing at the Suffolk County Jail, Kevin Ford was free to go on with his life. Conor had wasted more than a few hours wondering if he and Olivia were relaxing on some tropical beach somewhere.

He'd seen that look in Ford's eyes when he'd talked about Olivia. He had a suspicion Ford wouldn't stop at anything to make Olivia his, in the same way Conor wouldn't. But then Ford had the advantage of proximity. Conor cursed softly. He should never have let her go. Though his job had been in jeopardy and he didn't have anything to offer her, he still should have grabbed for the gold ring while he had the chance.

He yanked open the front door and stepped inside the dimly lit pub. The air was hazy with smoke and the jukebox played softly in the far corner. A few stragglers still sat at the bar and in the booths near the back. Conor slid onto a stool, then waved at Dylan who nursed a beer just a few stools away.

"You missed your party," Dylan said.

"What party?" Conor asked with a wry smile.

Sean stepped up and placed a half pint of Guinness in front of Conor. "Where were you? We've all been out looking for you. Geez, Con, you're a hard man to find when you don't want to be found."

"I had some business to take care of," Conor said. He reached out for the Guinness and took a long drink.

Sean wiped the bar around him with a damp towel, then tossed the towel over his shoulder. "Well, you had business here, too."

Conor shook his head wearily. "I wasn't in the mood for a party," he countered. In truth, all he wanted was to find Olivia. Unfortunately, he hadn't been able to make that happen.

"He's not talking about a party," Dylan explained. "He's talking about Olivia."

Conor's head snapped up at the mention of her name. "Olivia?"

Sean cocked his head toward the back of the bar. "Brendan's keeping her company at the dartboard. She's been waiting for most of the night."

"For me?" Conor asked.

"No, idiot," Sean muttered. "For his Holiness the Pope. If I were you, I'd get back there before Brendan has her completely charmed and she decides she came here for the wrong Quinn."

Conor sat frozen to his seat. What would he say to her? What would she say to him? He'd made so many mistakes already, an apology was probably in order. But after that, the only thing he could think to tell her was that he loved her. "It all comes down to this," he murmured. In just a few minutes, he'd know whether he'd found the woman he was meant to spend his life with or whether he'd made a mistake he'd regret for the rest of his life.

"Just tell her how you feel," Dylan suggested, as if he could read Conor's mind.

Conor had always been the one to provide sage advice to his younger brothers, but now he was on the receiving end of their advice and he wasn't sure he should trust them. Besides, what about all those family legends about the Mighty Quinns? Was he willing to trust his heart to a woman, to risk that she might someday walk out on him?

"She loves you, Con," Sean murmured. "She wouldn't have come here if that wasn't so. Don't be a jackass and mess this up. Besides, it's about time one of us tested that damn family curse. It might as well be you."

Conor pushed off the bar stool, took another long drink of his Guinness, then wiped his mouth on the back of his hand. He started toward the back of the bar, and though he'd walked that same path hundreds of times before, this time it felt like he was walking a mile, every step filled with doubt and insecurity.

He walked past Liam and Brian, who were deep into a game of eight ball. Both Brendan and Olivia had their backs to him as they aimed darts at the board mounted on the rear wall. Olivia was laughing and Brendan was teasing her. When they both went to reclaim their darts and count the score, Conor held his breath. And then she turned and faced him and their eyes met.

Everything and everyone around them suddenly faded into the background. He didn't hear what Brendan said and the music playing from the jukebox became just a jumble of sound. Instead, he heard her soft gasp, saw the light reflecting off her pale hair, smelled the scent of her perfume. It was all magnified a hundred times until his heart and soul was filled with her.

"Hi," he murmured.

"Hi," she replied.

Conor drew a shaky breath. "I've been looking for you. I went to your apartment and to the shop, but you weren't there."

"I was here," she said, glancing around nervously.

He swallowed hard, the words he wanted to say catching in his throat. "You look beautiful." It was all he could manage but it was the truth. He was stunned by the sight of her, shocked that his memories of her hadn't even come close to the reality of the woman before him. Conor silently vowed that he'd never depend on memories again.

He took a step toward her. "I wanted to find you because there are some things I need to tell you."

"There are some things I need to tell you," she countered.

"Those last few days when we were together, I—"

"I know," Olivia said. "They weren't about the job, were they?"

"How did you know?" Conor asked.

"Kevin Ford told me that he cut a deal the day after you visited him, nine days before the trial began. You got around to telling me I was safe four days before the trial. So I had to wonder, what was going on for the rest of that time. Why didn't you just take me home?"

Conor raked his hand through his hair, then tried to calm his nerves. "Olivia, I don't know any better way to put it than to just come out and say the words. I love you. Hell, I've probably loved you since the very moment you kicked me in the shin and called me a Neanderthal. And I'm sorry it's taken me so long to realize it, but I kept trying to convince myself that it was just part of the job. That my feelings of protectiveness were all mixed up with feelings I thought I had for you." He drew a long breath. "But now I know that's not true. I know how I feel and I don't want to live another day of my life without you."

Now that the words had started to come, Conor couldn't seem to stop them. He grabbed Olivia's hands and led her over to a booth, then slipped in opposite her. When they were both seated, he wrapped his fingers around hers and stared into her eyes.

"I suppose you're wondering how I know I love you," he continued.

"Not really," Olivia murmured. "I just—"

"Well, let me explain," he interrupted. "You see, when my mother left she just forgot all about us. We were her children and she just walked away. And I guess I always thought if it was so easy for our own mother to walk away, then it would be even easier for any other woman to do the same. Including you."

"I would never—"

"And when we first met," Conor said, "I tried to maintain my distance, but you needed me. And in the end, I think I needed you just as much." He took a quick breath, then continued on, certain that if he stopped talking she'd find some gentle way of rejecting him. He had to lay out his whole case and prove the truth of his words. If he didn't, she might just walk away. He drew her hands to his lips and kissed her fingertips. "You got inside of me, Olivia, and no woman has ever done that before. And I—"

"Can I just say something, please?" she asked in an impatient tone.

Conor froze, his lips just inches from her fingertips. This was it. She was going to brush aside everything he'd said and tell him that they could never have a future together. "All right."

A smile broke across her face and her eyes glittered with unshed tears. "Would you please stop talking and just kiss me?"

Stunned, he stared at her for a long moment. In that time, he saw all the emotion, all the love that he had for her, reflected in Olivia's eyes. With a low growl, Conor leaned over the table and did exactly as she requested. And as he kissed her, Conor knew that this woman would never bring him down. With every moment they spent together, he would become a better man. She loved him and with her love he felt as if he could rule the world.

He cupped her face in his hands and deepened the kiss until the need inside him grew to a soft ache. When they finally paused to draw breath, he gazed into her eyes. "Marry me," he murmured. "Make me the happiest man in the world."

"I will," Olivia said.

Conor laughed, then sat back in the booth. He'd expected an excuse, a plea to wait before they took such a serious step. After all, they'd known each other less than a month. But as Olivia smiled, he knew she was as anxious to begin their future together as he was, and they already knew enough to want that future to begin now. "Really? You'll marry me?"

She nodded. "I will marry you, Conor Quinn. And we'll live together and love together and I promise to give you handsome Irish sons and pretty Irish daughters." She reached out and softly touched his cheek. "And I promise that no matter what troubles come our way, I will never, ever leave you."

With that, Conor stood and slipped out of the booth, then tugged her out behind him. He couldn't resist pulling her into his arms and kissing her again, long and hard. When he was through, he glanced around to find his brothers all standing nearby. He laughed, then hugged Olivia to him. "I'm getting married."

"Oh, yeah?" Dylan shouted. "And where did you find a woman crazy enough to marry you?"

"The same place he found a woman willing to be a sister-in-law to a bunch of rowdy Irish brothers," Olivia said. "That is, if you'll have me."

The Quinn brothers gathered close, showering Olivia with their best wishes and a fair share of kisses as well. Conor stood back, watching the woman he'd come to love more than life itself, and the brothers who had been his life up until he'd met Olivia. And when all the congratulations were given, he grabbed his glass of Guinness from a nearby table and raised it above his head.

"To the Quinn family legend," he said.

His brothers grabbed their own glasses and held them up. "To the Quinn family legend."

Conor stared into Olivia's eyes, unable to believe that he'd won such a prize. "May you all find a woman as wonderful as Olivia, and may you all be laid low by your love for her. For a Mighty Quinn is nothing without a woman by his side."

They all took a drink of their Guinness and then Conor grabbed Olivia around the waist and kissed her again. Liam put a quarter in the jukebox and the strains of a lively Irish reel filled the bar. Conor swept Olivia into the dance, spinning her around and around until her face was flushed and she was breathless. And as they danced, he thought about all the dances they'd share in their future—the first dance together as man and wife, a dance on each of their anniversaries, a dance at the wedding of each of the children they would have.

He knew as long as he had Olivia at his side, in his arms, he would never regret a single moment of his life. A Mighty Quinn had found a mate and now that he'd found her, he'd wasn't about to let her go.

One Mighty Quinn has fallen,
and another one's at risk.
Don't miss watching Dylan's valiant attempts
to avoid the family curse.
Watch for

THE MIGHTY QUINNS: DYLAN,

available next month.

COMING SOON...

AN EXCITING
OPPORTUNITY TO SAVE
ON THE PURCHASE OF
HARLEQUIN AND
SILHOUETTE BOOKS!

*DETAILS TO FOLLOW
IN OCTOBER 2001!*

YOU WON'T WANT TO MISS IT!

PHQ401

*Harlequin truly does
make any time special. . . .
This year we are celebrating
weddings in style!*

A
Walk
Down
the Aisle
WEDDING CELEBRATION

To help us celebrate, we want you to tell us how wearing the Harlequin wedding gown will make your wedding day special. As the grand prize, Harlequin will offer one lucky bride the chance to **"Walk Down the Aisle"** in the **Harlequin wedding gown!**

There's more...

For her honeymoon, she and her groom will spend five nights at the **Hyatt Regency Maui.** As part of this five-night honeymoon at the hotel renowned for its romantic attractions, the couple will enjoy a candlelit dinner for two in Swan Court, a sunset sail on the hotel's catamaran, and duet spa treatments.

A HYATT RESORT AND SPA

Maui ▪ Molokai ▪ Lanai

To enter, please write, in, 250 words or less, how wearing the Harlequin wedding gown will make your wedding day special. The entry will be judged based on its emotionally compelling nature, its originality and creativity, and its sincerity. This contest is open to Canadian and U.S. residents only and to those who are 18 years of age and older. There is no purchase necessary to enter. Void where prohibited. See further contest rules attached. Please send your entry to:

Walk Down the Aisle Contest

In Canada	In U.S.A.
P.O. Box 637	P.O. Box 9076
Fort Erie, Ontario	3010 Walden Ave.
L2A 5X3	Buffalo, NY 14269-9076

You can also enter by visiting www.eHarlequin.com
Win the Harlequin wedding gown and the vacation of a lifetime!
The deadline for entries is October 1, 2001.

HARLEQUIN®
Makes any time special ®

PHWDACONT1

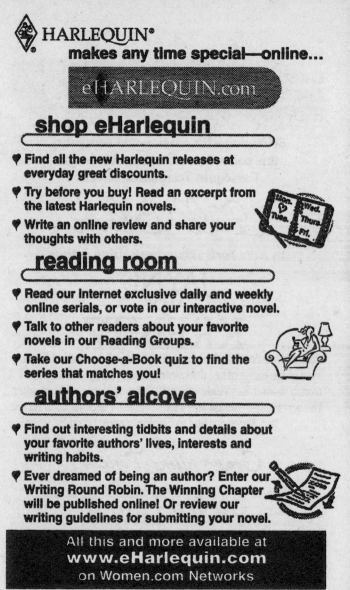

Brimming with passion and sensuality, this collection offers two full-length Harlequin Temptation novels.

Full Bloom

by *New York Times* bestselling author

JAYNE
—ANN—
KRENTZ

Emily Ravenscroft has had enough! It's time she took her life back, out of the hands of her domineering family and Jacob Stone, the troubleshooter they've always employed to get her out of hot water. The new Emily—vibrant and willful—doesn't need Jacob to rescue her. She needs him to love her, against all odds.

And

Compromising Positions

a brand-new story from bestselling author

VICKY LEWIS
THOMPSON

Look for it on sale September 2001.